KOUSINS
KAN'T KILL

Kousins Kan't Kill

Jerri Kay Lincoln

Ralston Store Publishing
P.O. Box 1684
Prescott, Arizona 86302

ISBN 978-1-938322-51-8

Professionally edited by:
Jennifer Hope
www.MesaVerdeMediaServices.com

The reader should note that the nutritional beliefs
and food choices in this book are those of the
characters and not necessarily those of the author or
publisher.

Printed in the USA.

Dedicated to the sleuth in all of us.

CHAPTER ONE

IT WAS QUIET in the Rutledge Historical Society building. The only sound was the soft whirr of the filter in the fish tank. Usually when I arrived at work, Petra would already be at her desk studying her online high school and college courses. Petra was my sixteen-year-old office companion—weird office companion, I might add. Weird but reliable. That was Petra. But today, my son Aiden had to be at school early, so here I was. Aiden was the best thing that had ever happened to me. The adoption wasn't final yet, but it would be soon. We had been together for only five months, and what a great five months it had been.

I smiled to myself remembering how cute he looked on Halloween. Dressed up like Sheriff Billy—including matching cowboy boots, matching Smokey Bear hat, matching shirt and pants, and an almost matching star— Aiden looked adorable. Sheriff Billy's star said Sheriff and Aiden's said Deputy. But Aiden was okay with that —at least after Billy had told him it was a *real* badge and not a make-believe one. I swear, Aiden stood up straight and walked with such a swagger that anybody would think he was the real thing—at least a short version of the real thing. Aiden was only seven.

And I should mention that Billy didn't walk with a swagger—anything but. He was very unaffected and straightforward. When I first met him, I thought he was an arrogant, power-hungry jerk—that, however, was from my ex-husband Eddie's perspective that I hadn't yet discarded. When I got to know Billy, though, I had found him kind, thoughtful, and extremely good looking. Did I mention that he was my boyfriend?

That almost didn't happen. When he came across me standing over a dead body and then threw me into jail, it didn't look good for the future of a relationship with him. But we mended that indiscretion and had been together ever since—which wasn't that long, really, but it was good. Billy was a good man. A really good man. He treated me and Aiden so well that sometimes I felt like I was living the dream.

Bingo, my dog, stood up from where he had been cuddled up with the cat and wagged his tail at me. Smiling, I petted him. It wasn't so long ago that I thought I had lost Bingo. Through a set of circumstances that Eddie, my husband at the time, had arranged, I had given Bingo to a neighbor who later moved to Phoenix. After I left Eddie, the neighbor, who had decided to move back east, came looking for me and gave me back my dog.

Between my son Aiden and my dog Bingo, life was good. And throw in a man like Billy, and I felt like I had it all. The cat jumped into my lap. When I stroked him, he purred. Rocky, named after his encounter with a raccoon, was the *house cat* at the Rutledge Historical Society. At first when I started working here, I hated him and was highly allergic. But we had worked out our differences. I kissed him on the top of his head and then sneezed, and ignored the itching in my eyes and nose. Most of our differences, anyway.

Leaning back in my chair, I looked at the painting over the fish tank. It was of the *original* Rutledge Historical Society building. Yes, it was the same building I sat in now, but the one in the picture was before a third of the building had been sectioned off for the Rutledge Koffee Korner Kafe. The original was a grand old building, two stories of mostly red brick with two broad windows on the bottom floor and three smaller windows on the top floor. A zigzag pattern of gray bricks above the top three windows made the building look really classy for its time.

But now, facing the building from the front, the left third of the building was painted bright yellow with stylized printing saying Rutledge Koffee Korner Kafe on it. The "R" in Rutledge was made to look like a K. It was deplorable what they had done to the beautiful old building. Someday I hoped that would be rectified to allow her to return to her old glory.

I took a sip of my coffee from my Unicorn Whisperer water bottle, which Aiden had gotten for me, and flipped on the computer to check my email. Another day, another dollar. Oh, wait. Not exactly. When I started this job, I was on my last dime, living out of a crummy motel just this side of a roach motel, driving a broken-down Karmann Ghia, and having to save my pennies for either a tank of gas or a meal. Not both, mind you, one or the other. But life had changed. Very much so.

Now I work here at the Rutledge Historical Society to have something to do. I'm not the country club or ladies society type, though I do like getting dressed up in my suits and heels every day. Today I wore a smart navy blue suit with a white blouse. Navy heels to match, of course.

I felt comfortable there, the work was more enjoyable than it was taxing, and I really liked Petra. She was a little weird with her tattoos and all, but she's a good person, and I could count on her.

My cousin Kasey, who worked next door at the Rutledge Koffee Korner Kafe, interrupted my pleasant reverie. The bell on the door jingled as she breezed right through with her bright yellow waitress uniform. She looked serious. Kasey never looked serious. I didn't think I had ever seen her without a smile on her face.

"Kasey! What's wrong?" I asked before she even had a chance to get all the way through the door.

"Oh, Lorry. I'm in trouble, so much trouble. Deep trouble."

Although I doubted it, her expression made me reconsider. Kasey was never in trouble. She had always done the right thing in school, had married her high school sweetheart, and now had two children and a happy marriage.

"Tell me. What's wrong?"

"When I went to the post office this morning, there was this dead guy on the floor. I know he was dead because there was blood all over, and a gun on the floor beside him that smelled like it had just been fired. I'm sure somebody saw me." She shook her head. "I'm in so much trouble."

I stood up and grabbed her hands. "Kasey! Please tell me you didn't pick up the gun to see if it had been fired." Nodding my head and raising my eyebrows, I continued, "You just got down on your knees and sniffed it, right? You didn't touch it, right?"

Tears slid down her cheeks, and she shook her head. "I picked it up to sniff it, because I thought it was important that I should know."

It was too much to hope for, I knew. Kasey had always been an airhead. Resigned, I shook my head and slumped back into my chair. "Oh, Kasey, I can't believe you did that. But I'm sure it will be all right. You found some random dead guy in the post office. Why would anyone think you would have any connection to him?" After I paused for a second, I asked, "You didn't do anything else stupid to the body, did you?" Yes, I asked her that. I'm a calls 'em as I sees 'em kind of person. And what I saw wasn't good, and I had to know how not good it was.

She nodded without looking at me. "I did."

"What?" I asked, exasperated. This was too much to believe, even for Kasey.

"I kissed him."

"Why would you kiss a *dead guy*? Someone you didn't even know!" I demanded.

Kasey lifted her head, tears still streaming down, and said, "Because I *did* know him; I was having an affair with him."

CHAPTER TWO

FEELING HORRIFIED BY what she had just told me, I tried to hide it from Kasey. Color me shocked. Absolutely, positively shocked. I had done some stupid things in my life, but I had never been unfaithful to a boyfriend or husband. Not that I had that many—boyfriends not husbands, that is—but still, it was something I would never do. Even when I knew that Eddie, my one ex-husband, had regular affairs with multiple women, I never did it. That may have made the situation *fair*, but it wouldn't have made it *right*. Still, I had been working on not being judgmental. Perhaps this was a test.

My mouth must have been hanging open, because when I finally recognized there was silence between us, Kasey spoke.

"I know, Lorry, you don't have to tell me that I shouldn't have. But I couldn't help myself. John was the only man I'd ever been with. I was"—she shrugged her shoulders—"you know, *curious*."

Nodding my head, still in disbelief, I asked, "So it was short-term then?"

Kasey shook her head and looked down. "Kind of. Only a year."

A year! She called a year *short-term*. And I thought she was so happily married. I should have gotten a clue a few months ago when she had told me she was on birth control pills even though John wanted another child. Of course she was on the pill—she couldn't risk getting pregnant with someone else's baby. "Wow, Kasey, I don't know what to say."

"Say you'll talk to Sheriff Billy on my behalf. I didn't kill him. I swear it."

"I'll talk to him, Kasey, but honestly, he has to do his job. Remember? He even put *me* in jail." It was a sad time for me when Billy had done that. It didn't make it any better that we weren't involved yet, because we were friends at the time. But, in his defense, he *did* find me standing over Eddie's dead body.

"Do what you can, Lorry. Please. I've gotta go back to work." She opened the door, jingling the bell, and slipped outside without saying goodbye.

Looking out the window, I watched as Kasey passed by on her way back to the cafe next door. Shaking my head, I took a deep breath to let everything she had told me soak in, and then I saw movement across the street. A sheriff's car—not Billy's—pulled up in front of the post office. The two deputies, Nick and Derek, jumped out with guns drawn. They ran into the post office while I watched, engrossed in the drama. Who would they pull out of there? And then I felt a sick feeling in the pit of my stomach. I knew *exactly* who they would pull out of there.

A minute later, Nick stepped out the door in front of Derek, who had Zackary James by the arm. Zack was in handcuffs. Nick, a few steps ahead, opened the back door of the car. Derek gave Zack a shove almost sending Zack toppling over. With those handcuffs on, I don't know how he maintained his balance, but somehow he did. That was mean, I thought. Nick put his hand on Zack's head as Zack entered the back seat of the car. Then Nick leaned in to attach the seat belt, closed the door, opened the front door, and took something out. The two deputies walked back into the post office. They came out a few minutes later, stretching yellow crime scene tape all across the front doors of the post office.

Derek retrieved something else out of the front of the car, which I recognized to be the forensic kit. They both had just stepped back inside the post office when Petra came in the front door in a barely controlled hysteria, knocking the bell into submission.

"Lorry, that was Zack in the car, wasn't it?" She had all her piercings intact, and her hair was a delicious shade of pink. Delicious if you were cotton candy.

"Yes, Petra, but I wouldn't worry about it. This will all get straightened out."

"Why is he in there? What did he do now?"

Now being the salient word. Zack, an old friend of Petra's, had led a troubled youth and had been in trouble many times. He had even been suspected of murder a few months ago. But he was a good kid who had grown up under trying circumstances and was now trying to better himself. Never for a second did I think Zack had killed Kasey's boyfriend. After what she had just told me, I would consider *her* more of a suspect than Zack. Still, Zack was the one with the record, so Zack was the one they would bring in.

Zack was at the post office because he worked there

now. He worked there days and took a couple of college classes at night. We even had him babysit for Aiden when Petra couldn't make it. I trusted him. Billy trusted him. It wouldn't take long for this to get straightened out. I hoped.

"Lorry! You're not answering me! What did he do? Please!" Petra interrupted my thoughts.

"Sorry, Petra, I was thinking about how far Zack has come in the last few months. He didn't do anything. But somebody was murdered in the post office."

"Who?"

"Well, um," I hesitated. Should I tell Petra or not? She was sixteen years old, but she was a very mature sixteen. And she'd find out soon enough anyway. "Kasey's boyfriend."

"Kasey? Your cousin Kasey? I thought she was happily married."

"So did I," I said. "So did I."

We looked out the window and saw the two deputies, one carrying a plastic evidence bag, enter the sheriff's car. Then it drove away with Zack in handcuffs in the backseat.

CHAPTER THREE

"TELL ME MORE. What happened?" Petra asked.

"I don't know more, Petra. Kasey came in here and told me she just found her boyfriend dead at the post office. She wanted me to tell Billy that she didn't do it."

"Are you going to?"

"I'll tell him what Kasey said. That's all I can do. Need I remind you what Billy did to *me* a few short months ago?"

Petra laughed. "I think he's more than made up for that now! You guys have been together every day since."

I lifted one shoulder in defense. "Not *every* day."

Petra laughed again then sobered quickly. "What do you think will happen to Zack?"

"Nothing. I think Billy will question him because he has to and then will release him. But Kasey has definitely got herself into trouble this time."

"Why do you say that?"

"Airhead Kasey picked up the gun to sniff it!"

"She picked up the gun? You're kidding. Do you believe her?"

"If I had to choose between her and Zack doing it, I

would go with Kasey. But honestly, I don't think she did it, either."

"Well if Zack didn't do it and Kasey didn't do it, who did?"

At that moment, the door opened and Kasey walked in again, still shaken. "Hi, Petra. Um—"

Noticing her hesitation to speak in front of Petra, I said, "It's okay, Kasey. I already told Petra."

Kasey nodded her head without malice and looked at me. "Did you tell Billy yet that I didn't do it?"

"I haven't seen him. Shouldn't we wait until he takes you in to talk to you?"

Kasey put her hands on either side of her face. "Oh, no! I can't go in! No, no, no. That would never do! John would find out!"

"Kasey, you touched the gun. Your fingerprints are on the murder weapon. You *will* be taken in. There's no way around it."

Panicky, she looked around. "Then I have to run away!"

"No, Kasey, you can't run away. You're going to go in and explain exactly what happened."

Tears slid down Kasey's face, and she emitted a small gasp when the sheriff's car pulled up in front of the Rutledge Koffee Korner Kafe and stopped. Nick exited the vehicle and opened the back door to let Zack out. While Zack walked across the street to the post office, Derek walked into the cafe.

"There, Petra, they already let Zack go. No worries."

"But they went next door to get *me!*" whimpered Kasey. Then she turned toward the back to run, but Petra blocked her path.

"Running away isn't the answer, Kasey. You need to

face this. Just explain how everything came down. If you didn't do it, then you have no reason to feel afraid. Do you have any idea who could have done this?"

She looked up as if gathering her thoughts. "He had an ex-girlfriend." Kasey nodded her head. "And I know that she called him more than once in the past week. I can't think of anyone else." Then she collapsed in on herself with the tears streaming down her face. Looking up, she added, "Well, it could have been his wife."

Then the deputies burst through the door of the historical society, and Kasey's silent tears turned into sobs. Derek grabbed her by the upper arm and twisted it behind her back. It looked like it hurt.

"Hey!" I said. "What happened to innocent until proven guilty?"

"We'll just see if her fingerprints are on the gun we found at the scene," he said without looking at me.

He put the handcuffs on her and when he fastened them, Kasey said, "Ouch."

"Hey, can't you loosen them? She's not going anywhere."

Derek ignored me and opened the door that had slammed shut when they grabbed her. Nick checked her handcuffs and loosened them a notch or two.

"Thank you," Kasey said quietly. Then, as they led her through the door, she turned to me. "Lorry, please call John for me. Let him know what's going on. You know. Everything."

Nick began reading her her rights, and they disappeared out the door. Derek put his hand on her head to get her into the car and then shoved her into the back seat.

"Petra? Did you see that? And what he did to her in

12

here? Isn't that police brutality?"

"It did look pretty mean, didn't it?" Petra stood in front of me. "Did you hear the last thing she said before the deputies came in? That it might have been his wife?"

Exhaling loudly, I shook my head. "I can't believe little goodie-two-shoes Kasey, who never did a thing wrong in her life, not only had a boyfriend, but *he* was married, too. I can't believe it."

"It is hard to believe, isn't it? Did you know that innocent was derived from the Latin *innocens* meaning harmless, inoffensive?"

"No, Petra"—I slowly exhaled to keep my composure —"I didn't know that."

"So who you going to check out first?"

"Petra! I'm not the detective on this case, Billy is! Let him figure it out."

"But you've already solved two other murders!"

"They were personal. This is different."

"Lorry, Kasey is your cousin! This is personal, too! You *have* to figure it out!"

I pretended that I was hitting my head against the wall. "Not again. Please not again."

CHAPTER FOUR

THE HIGH SCHOOL included two red brick two-story buildings angled together with a courtyard in between. Although I couldn't see the courtyard from the front where I entered, I remembered it had picnic benches on a grassy area. The grassy area was the butt of controversy when I went to school there because of watering it to keep it green. I wondered if it was still there or if they had given in to political pressure. Remembering how sweet that grass felt when I put my feet on it during lunchtimes when I was in high school made me sigh with satisfaction. That was probably my best high school experience. It would be a shame to do away with it. Although I didn't go to school there anymore and hadn't for years, I still hoped the grass was there.

Entering through the big front doors into an open area brightly lit by the front windows, I took a deep breath at the agreeable surroundings. I didn't feel any of that residual high school angst from when I went to school there. It may have been more than ten years ago, but high school can have a hold on you for a long time after you leave—especially if your time there wasn't pleasant.

And I had plenty of high school angst to go around. It wasn't that I didn't get good grades while I was there—I did—and it wasn't that I suffered so much, at least any more than any other teenager, but I was never one of the *in*-crowd. And it wasn't even that I wanted to be, but they let you know all the time you weren't one of them. Small high schools in small towns can be like that. But it's all in the past now.

The administration offices were to the right, and I walked in. Smiling at the receptionist, whom I didn't know, I stepped up to the counter. So many times, students who used to attend high school return as teachers or janitors or office staff. That might have been true, but she was no one that I had gone to school with.

"I'm here to see John Brannigan, please." John was Kasey's husband, and he was about to get some terrible news. "My name is Lorry Lockharte." She was too young to know about the *Rutledge Lockhartes*, and it had probably been too long for it to matter anyway.

My mother was Camilla Lockharte who owned the Lockharte mansion on Hillside Terrace, the rich part of town. When she died several years ago, her attorneys had told me she had given all her money to charity and had left me nothing. They lied. And I was so glad they did. I was married to Eddie then, and he was a degenerate gambler. It wouldn't have taken long for him to run through that money, and I, idiot that I was back then to go along with whatever he wanted, would have let him. My mother hated Eddie and knew how dysfunctional my relationship with him was. She was a wise woman. After Eddie was gone, I had inherited my mother's multimillion dollars.

The Rutledge Lockhartes were famous around here because my father, before he died, had built many of the homes on Hillside Terrace. He had bought all the land and had the road bulldozed and paved. Our house, where I grew up, was the first house on the street.

"Do you have an appointment?" the young woman asked.

"No, but he'll know me," I said. "And he'll want to see me," I added. That wasn't really true. What I had to tell him would not make him happy at all.

She nodded, picked up the telephone, and buzzed him. I heard her say, "Lorry Lockharte here to see you, John."

It was a small town and everybody was known by their first name. There were no phony airs of propriety here.

"He'll be right out."

"Thank you."

When John came out a few minutes later, he had a broad smile on his face that faded when he saw my sober expression. "Come into my office, Lorry." He was wearing a blue button-down shirt with a blue and white striped tie that wasn't securely fastened. So he looked professional but relaxed. Small-town America required you had to look the part, but not necessarily live it. Comfort was everything.

I knew where his office was, and he stepped aside so I could walk in before him. When we arrived, he walked straight to his desk, so I turned around and closed the door. The room was medium-sized, perfect for the principal of the high school. On the walls in front of and behind him were his educational achievements and a picture of a San Francisco Peaks snow scene. A large picture of Kasey and their two children, Lily and

Zandor, adorned his desk. The desk itself was large, metal, utilitarian, and functional—exactly what a school would provide for a principal. Besides the desk blotter calendar covered with papers in front of him, the inbox/outbox holder on the upper corner, and the picture of his family, the desk was immaculate—which was in stark contrast to his home.

"Lorry, what is it?"

"Kasey is at the sheriff's station."

"Why? What happened? Is she okay?"

"It's not good, John. She's suspected of murder."

"Murder? That's crazy! Whoever would Kasey murder? And why? Kasey might talk your ear off, but murder? No way." He shuffled the papers on his desk for something to do.

And all this time I thought he didn't notice how much she talked. "John, she had a boyfriend."

He looked up, and I saw a single tear well up in his eye and run down his face. "I know."

My heart bled for the guy. John Brannigan was tall, broad, with a crew cut, and a military bearing. He was one of the good guys, and he didn't deserve this. I felt bad for him.

Before I had a chance to tell him that the boyfriend was the one who was murdered, he continued without looking at me. "I found the birth control pills, and I knew there was more to it than her not wanting another child. Especially because I thought she *did* want another child. So I followed her a few times and finally caught them together."

"You didn't say anything?"

He shook his head. "Why? If she really loved me, she would come back to me, and if not, then the sooner I found out the better. What does *he* have to do with Kasey being in jail?"

"She's not in jail yet, but I'm sure she will be. The boyfriend is the one who was murdered, and Kasey was stupid enough to pick up the murder weapon"—before he had a chance to ask me why, although knowing Kasey, he might not have asked—"to sniff it to see if it was recently fired."

"Oh, Kasey!" More tears streamed down his face. "I can't believe you got yourself involved in all this." He shook his head.

"I'm sure when she got involved with him she didn't know he'd end up getting murdered." I felt the need to defend her.

"Oh, of course not, but knowing Kasey, she would pick the one guy who *would* end up that way." He pulled a box of Kleenex out of a drawer and put it on his desk. It was probably for the times when he suspended or expelled students, and he took one and dabbed at his eyes. "What can I do?"

Since I had been involved with Billy, I knew a thing or two about how everything worked down at the sheriff's station. And don't you mention my brief time there, because I wasn't there long enough to learn much of anything. All I know I've learned since then. Really.

"There's nothing you can do right now." I looked at my watch. "They will fingerprint her and question her. By the time they finish questioning her, they will have checked the fingerprints on the gun. As you can imagine, that's not good at all. Until they come up with another suspect, she's it."

John kept shaking his head back and forth and saying, "Oh, no, oh, no, oh, no."

I reached out my hand and patted his. "Don't worry, John. Billy will find out who did this."

John looked up suddenly. "Lorry, would you look into it for Kasey? And for me? I know—"

He was about to say how I had solved two prior murders, so I held up my hand. "John, it's not my place."

He dabbed at his eyes again with the Kleenex, but the tears kept on sliding down his face. "Please, Lorry? Please?"

How could I say no to an unhappy tear-stained face like that?

CHAPTER FIVE

WHEN I RETURNED to the historical society, I parked in back and walked inside. It surprised me to find Billy standing at Petra's desk talking to her. Billy and Petra were friends of long standing, back from when Petra, as a small child, would accompany her father to the local bars. Her father would then wind up in the drunk tank with Petra silently sobbing at the sheriff's station. Billy was a deputy then and would comfort her. And now, Billy paid Petra's online college tuition—not an easy feat to accomplish, because her father wanted no charity regardless of whether it benefited his daughter.

"Lorry!" Billy said as I walked up. "I was hoping you'd get here so we could talk. I only have a minute, though, because I need to take the tape off from across the street." He hugged me and kissed me on the lips.

"I went to see John," I told him.

Billy nodded and we walked together into my front office. He pointed at the post office, which I could see out my window. "People are driving by craning their necks wondering when it will open."

"What's happening with Kasey?" I asked.

"That's what I wanted to talk to you about. You know she picked up the gun?"

"Yeah, I couldn't believe she did that."

"It's worse than that. She tried to wipe the prints off and missed one. You know that makes her look guilty."

I frowned and shook my head. "She didn't tell me that part."

"She looks guilty as hell, Lorry."

"Oh, come on, Billy. You know Kasey couldn't have done this."

"Just because she's your cousin doesn't mean that she can't kill."

"Yeah, I guess."

"It's not good, Lorry. And Zack identified her at the scene." He moved his head from one side to the other. "Although he said that he didn't think she did it. Not that his word matters, you understand."

"Yeah, I get it. She didn't have any gun powder residue on her hands, though, did she?" Part of my criminal knowledge came from my relationship with Billy, and part of it came from when I was accused of murder. Billy, himself, not that long ago had checked my hands and belongings for gun powder residue.

"No, she didn't, but one of the deputies found gloves in the garbage. Whoever did it was smart. They used knit gloves with a vinyl glove over it, so there are no fingerprints."

"Kasey would never think of that. And if she used gloves, then why would her fingerprints still be on the gun?"

He nodded. "Yeah, that doesn't make sense. Actually, I don't think she did it, but we have to go through the procedure." Shrugging, he said, "You know."

21

"Will she go to county?" I meant Coyote Moon, the next city over, because they had a regular jail and courthouse, and that's where all Rutledge's big cases were tried. Not that there were that many, but still.

"She's on her way there now."

"Who's driving her?"

"They both are. Why?"

"Because Derek got a little heavy handed with both Zack and Kasey. He pushed Zack—who was already handcuffed—almost to the ground, and he was rough with Kasey and made her cuffs way too tight. Nick had to loosen them."

"Oh, that makes sense, though. The victim is Derek's sister's husband. For him, it's personal. But I'll talk to him." He leaned forward and kissed me again. "Gotta go, sweetie. I'll be back sometime later. Bye."

After I watched him go, I walked to Petra's office, on the other side of the wall from mine. "Petra, would you mind holding down the fort? There's something I have to do."

She smiled at me, blinked, and tilted her head. "I heard Billy kiss you. I knew he liked you!"

Petra had been telling me from the beginning that Billy liked me, and now she never lost an opportunity to rub that in. She was, after all, sixteen years old. "Yes, yes, I know, you were right. But he took long enough to show it!"

"You got him hooked now, though." Her smile faded. "Is it something to do with the murder?"

"Yup."

"Then go ahead. I'm good here. With all the excitement in town, probably no one will show up anyway."

"Thanks, Petra!"

Petra was a serious student, and I didn't like to inconvenience her more than I had to. She was finishing her final two years of high school while at the same time completing her first two years of college. It was a lot of work. But sometimes, days went by without the Rutledge Historical Society even getting one visitor.

Rutledge wasn't exactly the historical center of the West. Probably the most impressive event that ever happened here was when Wyatt Earp and Doc Holliday stopped on their way to Prescott. And that was just hearsay. It might never have happened. But that's the rumor, anyway. Do I believe it? Naw. That rumor has commercial advantages. Call me a cynic, but I think some creative city father with foresight just made it all up.

CHAPTER SIX

I DROVE HOME, hurried inside, and changed clothes into my—what Billy would call—civvies. They comprised jeans, a flannel shirt, and something I rarely wore: tennis shoes. I hung up my work clothes on hangers, stuffed a couple of large, black garbage can bags into my pockets, and carried the hangers back outside. After locking the door, I stood at my doorstep a moment to listen. It was late fall. Most of the trees had lost their leaves, but there were still several stragglers in the trees by my house. At the encouragement of the gentle breeze, the leaves shook and sounded like a quiet audience applauding its approval. I took that as a sign I was doing the right thing.

Billy had already removed all the tape blocking the post office, so I parked in front. People hadn't realized that it was open yet, so I found a parking spot easily. I walked in and luckily ran into Zack—lucky because he was exactly who I was looking for.

"Hi, Lorry. Did you see them cart me out of here?" He looked ashamed.

Smiling at him, I said, "Yes, and I saw them bring you

back! I knew you didn't do it."

He smiled back at me. "Thank you for believing in me, Lorry. You know you've made all the difference in my life." Holding the broom in his hand, he said, "I wouldn't be where I am today if not for you." It seemed a little ironic, but he was talking more about straightening his life out and less about being janitor at the post office.

"Did you happen to dump the garbage yet?" I asked, motioning toward a garbage can beside the table with pens attached. Although the pens usually didn't work, that didn't stop people from trying them all the time. The garbage can had that swivel top that moved back and forth when you put trash in.

"No, not yet. I was going to as soon as I finish sweeping. Running behind today, you know?"

"Of course. Do you know if the deputies went through it?"

"I'm pretty sure they took the gloves off the top and left the rest."

"Good, that's what I was hoping for. Would it be all right if I took it into the back and went through it? It probably wouldn't be a good idea to do it out here."

Zack tucked his chin and smiled. "I wondered what you were doing dressed like that, Lorry. I know you should be all dressed up at work today."

"My good stuff is in the car." Pointing to my clothes, I said, "I just changed for the dumpster diving. Do you think it would be all right?"

"Sure, let me carry it to the back for you."

Zack carried the can into the back, took off the lid, pointed to it, and said, "Have at it, Lorry."

"Thanks, Zack." He was such a good kid. I felt

25

gratified that he was finally on the right path with life. It would have been frustrating and anticlimactic if he had gone back to doing the wrong thing after I defended him several months ago.

I opened one of the black garbage bags I had brought and reached into the garbage bin. There was a lot of junk mail in there, but I examined each piece carefully before throwing it into the bag. Although I didn't know what I was looking for, I knew I would know it if I found it. Five minutes and a quarter of the can later, I hadn't found a thing except some bubblegum stuck between two pieces of junk mail. I had to pry it loose to make sure nothing was on either side of the gum. No luck, just yuck.

Continuing on, several minutes passed before I got past the halfway mark. Nothing, nothing and more nothing, and I was getting frustrated. What was I even doing here? If the forensic deputies didn't think it was important enough to go through, what was I doing going through garbage anyway? Pawing through, I got to the three-quarter mark, when I saw something crumpled down at the bottom of the bin. I reached through the junk mail to pick it up.

After uncrumpling it, I read, *J, Please meet me an hour early. I have something important to tell you. Love, K.* I held it in my hand reading it over and over again. This felt like it was it—the thing I was looking for. Of course, if Kasey's boyfriend's name was Thomas, then it wouldn't fit at all. The note wasn't dirty at all—no bubblegum, no coffee stains, no mustard—so I stuck it in my pocket, and kept looking through the trash. No sense in being hasty, especially since I didn't even know the guy's name. When I got to the bottom of the trash without another shred of evidence or whatever you want to call it, I stood up and stretched.

Zack came in then. "You got to the bottom. Find what you're looking for?"

"I don't know. Do you know the guy's name who was killed?"

Zack's eyebrows went up. "No, but I can find out for you!"

"No, Zack, that's okay. I can find out from Billy."

Lines formed on Zack's forehead. "Sheriff Billy didn't really think I did it, did he?"

I put my hand on his shoulder. "Zack, if Billy thought you did it, you wouldn't be standing here right now, would you?"

The lines disappeared, and the hint of a smile appeared on his face. "No, I guess not."

"Neither of us thought you did it, Zack. Kasey said she didn't, but I'm still not convinced about her. *You*, I was sure about."

Zack shook his head. "Oh, I don't think she did it, Lorry. I heard her come in—you know, she's in here a lot in the mornings so I recognize her footsteps. And I think the guy was already dead. I never heard a gunshot or anything."

A gunshot. That's something I had never considered. "What time did you come in to work?"

"Seven. Same as always."

"Maybe it had already happened then."

"That's what I think. Kasey usually gets here around seven-thirty."

I nodded and then leaned down to dump the trash back into the bin. It was heavier than it looked.

"Oh, Lorry, you don't have to do that. I'll just chuck it

inside the bag—unless you want the bag back." He raised his eyebrows to me. Zack wasn't joking; he was being sincere.

"No, Zack, go ahead. You can keep the bag! Thanks for letting me go through the garbage. I appreciate it."

"Did you find anything worth your trouble?"

"That's yet to be seen," I said, patting the note in my pocket, but not mentioning it. Smiling, I said, "Goodbye, Zack," and walked into the lobby and out the door to my car.

CHAPTER SEVEN

THE RUTLEDGE HISTORICAL Society was just down the street from the post office, but I didn't want to block a parking place in front. So I started my car, turned it around at the dead end on End Street, and pulled around the corner and down the alley to park behind the society. Billy's sheriff's car was back there. That made me smile. Billy always made me smile.

I grabbed the hangers with my clothes, opened the door to the society, and walked into the back. Replacing the chain on the *No Admittance* sign, I started down the hallway. When I appeared at Petra's desk, Billy sat in front of it, talking to Petra.

"Lorry! I didn't hear you coming! *What* are you dressed in? No heels?"

I held up my clothes and without answering I slipped my purse into the bottom drawer of my desk and turned around. Billy was standing when I walked by Petra's office. "Be right back. I'll explain everything." Then I walked into the small bathroom and closed the door. After changing clothes, I retrieved the now not-so-crumpled note and walked back to my office. Billy was already in there, sitting at my desk. He jumped up when he saw me and hugged and kissed me.

"What?" I asked, "You can't kiss me unless I'm dressed up?"

Billy laughed and pointed to my feet. I hadn't even thought to bring my heels back to work with me, so I was still in my tennis shoes. "Oops," I said.

He wrapped his arms around me and pulled me from side to side. Then he kissed me again and said, "I love you no matter what you wear."

"And I love you even in your Smokey Bear hat!"

"So what were you doing in those clothes? Where were you?"

"I was at the post office. Look what I found." I held out the note to him and then pulled it back. "Wait. What's the victim's name?"

"Charles Jones, known as Chuck. Why?"

Frowning, I sat down and handed him the note. "Because I found this. Addressed to J from K. I thought maybe it was from Kasey to her boyfriend."

Billy shook his head. "Where'd you get this?" He turned the note over and then sniffed it.

That's what I call a thorough investigator! "In the garbage at the post office. I thought it could be relevant."

"Not unless Kasey called him Jerk, which I don't think she would! Kasey's not like that. I don't think it means anything, Lorry. Thanks for trying though." He crumpled the note and handed it back to me.

"Hmmm, I'll ask Kasey." Instead of putting it in the garbage can beside my desk, I opened the desk drawer and dropped the crumpled note inside.

Billy took my hand in his. His hand was big, just like the rest of him. He was six feet four inches of absolute hunk. "Look, Lorry, didn't we already have this discussion? *I'm* the sheriff, and you're my *girlfriend*, not my helper. Let the boys and me do our jobs. We can handle this."

"But it's my cousin Kasey. I have to do something. I can't just sit here with her languishing away in the Coyote Moon jail."

Billy laughed. "Lorry! It's Coyote Moon, not some third-world country! She'll be fine until morning, then she'll have a hearing."

"What happens then?"

"They'll set bail, and she can leave until the trial comes up. But I'm sure I'll find the real murderer before the trial happens."

"And if you don't?" I asked.

Billy shook his head. "Then it's not good for Kasey. She picked up the gun and then tried to wipe her prints off of it. It makes her look guilty. I can't pretend that it's not serious, Lorry, because it is."

"Poor Kasey. Poor airhead Kasey. What's next then?"

"I'm going over to talk to Charles Jones's wife."

I grimaced. "That's gotta be rough telling her that her husband was murdered and his mistress is in jail for the crime."

Billy sighed. "Luckily, I don't have to do that part. Since it's Derek's sister, he volunteered to tell her the details, but I'll be the one questioning her. With your cousin's life at stake, I didn't want to let a rookie do the questioning."

"Thanks, Billy. I appreciate that."

Billy pulled me to my feet and wrapped his arms around me again. "I knew you would! What do I get for that?" He kissed me lightly on the lips and raised his eyebrows.

"How about dinner and a game of Uncle Wiggly with Aiden?"

"Oh, thank you for reminding me. I'm going to—" The microphone attached to his shirt made a sound, and he keyed the mike. "Sheriff Billy here."

"Billy, it's Derek. I took care of it. I told my sister and questioned her, and I have all the information here for you."

Since I could hear every word, and since Billy had just told me that *he* was going to question the wife himself, I raised my eyebrows and looked at him.

He frowned. "Derek! I told you not to question her! I told you that you were to inform her only and leave the questioning to me. I was very clear on that." Billy spoke into the microphone, and I could tell that he was trying his best to control his anger.

"Well, Billy, now you don't have to, because I already took care of it." Derek's voice sounded light and almost taunting.

"Too bad for your sister then, because I'm going over there right now to question her."

There was a moment's hesitation, and then Derek came on the speaker again. "Sorry, Billy, but she was leaving after I finished questioning her. But you have my notes. I'm sure you'll find them satisfactory."

"Fine, then. I'll see you in fifteen minutes to go over your notes with you. I have to finish here before I get back to the office."

"Oh, you're at the historical society? *Again?*"

Billy looked at me, shook his head, and pointed to the speaker. "Derek, we'll talk about this when I see you in fifteen."

"What is up with that guy? What a jerk!" I said.

"He's just getting worse and worse." Billy frowned again.

"So you're going to accept his notes?"

Billy smiled an ironic smile. "No, of course not. But unless I agreed to go directly to the office, he would have called his sister and told her to leave the house. I'm not an idiot. I'm going over there right now."

"Do you already have her address or you want me to look it up here?" I motioned to the computer.

Billy patted his pocket. "It's here. I'll call you later." He gave me a quick kiss and disappeared down the hall toward the back door.

CHAPTER EIGHT

USUALLY, AIDEN WALKED the short distance from his school to the historical society. There were no streets to cross, and he had been doing it from long before I ever met him. But before I left John's office, John had asked if I could pick Lily up from school and have her spend the night. He said he could pick up and take care of Zandor —their infant named after a Weather Channel storm that never happened—but he didn't know what to say to Lily. John had enough on his mind right now, with the knowledge of Kasey having an affair and now in jail for the guy's murder. Having Lily spend the night was no hardship at all. And Aiden loved her. She was his best friend.

So I left the society in the capable hands of Petra and drove to Aiden and Lily's school. John had called Pamela Reilly, the principal, to say I was picking up Lily. When I pulled up in front of the school, Pamela was on the front steps with her arms around Lily. Aiden was on the other side of Lily with one arm draped around her. When Pamela saw me, she walked the two of them to the car. I saw that Lily was crying, so I jumped out of the car to try to comfort her.

The poor kid went from Pamela's arms into mine with Aiden still making contact. It was like he wanted her to know he was there for her. That was typical Aiden. He took his job of being a friend seriously.

"Aunt Lorry, the kids said my mommy is a murderer."

"She's not, Lily. Don't worry. It will be okay."

"She's not? Really? Are you sure? Because the kids said that it was her gun that killed the guy."

I looked at Pamela, who was still standing there, and I indicated with my shoulders and my expression that I wondered how they got that information so quickly. Pamela mouthed the words "the internet," and of course that was right. It was a modern school with computers in every room. And this was big news for Rutledge, Arizona. *Local married woman kills boyfriend.*

Kissing Lily on the head, I said, "Lily, your mom never had a gun. She did not kill him."

"Lily, they did the same thing to me when they said *my* mommy was a murderer," said Aiden.

Lily nodded through her tears. "I remember, Aiden."

It had only been a few months ago that Aiden went through this exact thing. Billy had given him a lesson on handling bullies, and he handled it well ever since.

"I'll keep them away from you, Lily. I'll protect you," said Aiden. He patted her on the back.

"You did good, Aiden. But it still bothers me they think that," said Lily.

"It's not true, Lily. You have to ignore them." Aiden continued patting her back. "I love you."

"Come on, Lily. Let's go home now." I opened the back door of the car and tried to get Lily to get in, but she clung to me. Quietly, I said, "Aiden," and motioned for him to get in.

He nodded and jumped into the back seat with Bingo, scooting over to give Lily room. But she wouldn't budge. She was attached to me like a barnacle on a ship. Aiden saw what was happening, so he scooted back over and reached for her hand. Softly, he said, "Come on, Lily, it will be all right. We can go to my house and play."

"I want to go home," Lily said between sobs.

Loosening her arms around me, I knelt down so I could look into her eyes. "Lily, listen. Your mom isn't there. You are going to stay with me and Aiden tonight, okay? We'll have pizza. You and Aiden can play. How 'bout that?"

"I want to go home," she sobbed.

Not knowing what else to do, I sat in the back seat of the car next to Aiden and pulled Lily onto my lap. "Come here, sweetie. You'll be fine. You'll get through this just like Aiden did. Because I wasn't guilty and neither is your mommy. Kids can be cruel. But Aiden can help you and teach you how to deal with them. You don't have to be afraid or ashamed. Everything will be all right." I rocked her while I talked.

When her sobs finally subsided, I slid out from beneath her, hooked her into the seat belt, and left her to Aiden's caresses. I looked back after I got into the driver's seat, and she had her head on Aiden's shoulder and was petting Bingo.

The trouble was I didn't know if it would be all right or not. Kasey *probably* didn't do it. But her picking up the gun to see if it had been fired sounded like a pretty lame excuse. Knowing Kasey, it was probably true. I did find it odd, though, that she tried to wipe off the fingerprints and didn't tell me. Kasey, with her constant chatter, usually didn't leave out any details. Maybe she forgot to mention it to me. That was probably it. With everything going on, and her so stressed out about her boyfriend getting murdered, she probably just forgot.

Her boyfriend. I thought that so casually like it was an okay thing. It wasn't okay. She had a good marriage to a good man. How could she do that to John? How could she do that to her children? Shaking my head, I thought that I couldn't judge someone when I didn't know all the facts. There were people who probably thought Eddie and I had a good marriage. They would have had to be blind, but, still, they might have thought that. And as much as I wanted to, I couldn't judge what Kasey had done—at least I shouldn't.

CHAPTER NINE

LILY WAS A wild child. Kasey and John didn't believe in disciplining their children, and Lily ran wild all the time. When Aiden was at their house, Aiden ran wild. It didn't take me long to realize that trying to make him behave while he was over there wasn't good for anyone. He would have done it—but it wasn't fair of me to ask him. When Lily was at our house, she was a little subdued, but not much. Either Aiden or I had to keep reminding her that at our home, children don't behave like that.

So seeing Lily on the couch crying, with Aiden sitting close beside her, one arm around her and holding her hand, bothered me. Aiden was talking to her soothingly, trying to get her to calm down. I thought something else might work better, so I tried to get Aiden's attention without Lily noticing. He looked up and when I motioned for him to go outside, he understood.

Sweet Aiden kissed Lily on the cheek and slid off the couch. He took both of her hands and tried to coax her off the couch. "Come on, Lily. Let's go outside and play."

Without looking up, she said, "I don't want to play."

Aiden, in all his wisdom that belied his unworldly seven years old, said, "Come on, Lily. I want to go outside, and I don't want to go alone. Please come out and keep me company. I'd like you there with me."

She looked up at him, tears still streaming down her face, and said, "Okay," while he pulled her up from the couch. Then he took her hand and started skipping down the hallway with her. She didn't skip at first, but when she couldn't keep up with him, she did. They went out the back door and five minutes later, I could hear Lily yelling outside. Good. She was back to her loud, wild self. That was a good sign. But the poor kid still had a lot to go through in the coming days.

I retrieved my cell phone from my purse and tapped in Billy's number. Just when I thought it was going to voicemail, he answered.

"Hi, Billy. . . . Yeah, I forgot to tell you that John asked me to pick up Lily and bring her home with me tonight. She's a mess. Poor kid. Hey, what happened with the guy's wife? Was she there when you got there, or had Derek already warned her away? . . . Oh, okay. . . . Listen, I wanted to tell you that I don't think it would be a good idea for you to come over too early tonight— maybe after the kids go to bed? . . . Yeah, you remember how Aiden reacted when— . . . Yeah, right! She doesn't. . . . So I'll save some pizza for you? . . . All right. I'll call you after I put them down for the night. . . . Love you, too. Bye."

There, I was glad Billy understood. I didn't think it was a good idea for him to be around Lily tonight. She might blame him for what happened to her mom—and how could she not blame him? Lily wasn't old enough to understand all the dynamics of what had happened.

But knowing what a blabbermouth Kasey is, Lily would probably know soon enough what her mother was doing and who the guy was who was killed. The problem was, if Lily knew, then Aiden would know. And seven was too young to know that kind of dark stuff about people. But aside from keeping Aiden away from Lily—which I couldn't even if I wanted to, since they went to the same school—there was no way to keep it from him. I would just see how it all went and then deal with the issues as they came up.

In the meantime, there was pizza. Although it was too early to eat dinner—wait, why was it too early?—I decided that I would call and order the pizza. Walking into the kitchen, I stood by the kitchen window, with the yellow and red striped curtains that I pulled back during the day, and picked up the phone that was on the wall. Truth be told, cell phones annoyed me, and I preferred what were now referred to as "land lines." In the *olden days*, everyone called them telephones or wall phones. I don't know why I called Billy from my cell—it seemed the right thing to do at the time.

As I waited for the pizza place to answer, I gazed at the house that I loved. The kitchen had a breakfast bar separating it from the living room, but it also had a small kitchen table—small, but big enough for four. My living room was spacious with a couch and a couple of easy chairs, and a television not connected to cable. Of course, every spare inch of wall space was devoted to bookshelves for both Aiden and me. When we weren't reading, which was what we normally did, we occasionally watched movies. Aiden may prefer adult books to read, but he loved kiddie movies, and admittedly, I enjoyed them, too.

I was not going to feel guilty about ordering pizza so early. This seemed like a good solution. If we ate early, then maybe I could put the kids to bed early, and Billy could come over early. Besides just wanting to spend time with him, I wanted to know what happened with the wife of the dead guy. Oh, was that disrespectful? Okay, the deceased. Although, a guy who was messing around on his wife, maybe deserves to be disrespected. But then again, since Kasey was messing around on her husband, shouldn't she be disrespected, too? This nonjudgment thing was much harder than just thinking the two of them were both contemptible idiots.

CHAPTER TEN

BY THE TIME the pizza was delivered—cold—it was almost five o'clock. I heated it up in the oven, because Aiden said if you heat it in the microwave it ruined the crispness of the crust. He was right, of course, but the microwave was so much quicker. We always got pepperoni pizza because it was our favorite, but Lily insisted on black olive and green pepper, so I ordered two. When we ate, Aiden opted for the black olive and green pepper so that Lily wouldn't feel alone. That kid has the biggest heart!

After we ate, we played a couple of games of Uncle Wiggly and Chutes and Ladders, and then I set up the cot in Aiden's room for Lily. I tucked them in at seven o'clock, and although I heard them talking, I knew they would settle in and fall asleep soon enough. Emotionally, it was a tough day for Lily, and I'm sure it had taken a lot out of her. Still, I waited to call Billy until eight o'clock.

Billy hadn't eaten, so I heated up the pizza—in the microwave this time—and sat at the table while he ate. He wanted to try the black olive and green pepper but then finished the pepperoni. While he ate, I told him how upset Lily was because the kids at school were taunting her. And I added how supportive Aiden was, and Billy nodded. He knew what a great kid Aiden was. When he finished eating, he washed his hands in the kitchen sink, and we retired to the living room to talk about the murder.

We sat on the couch, and Billy put his arm around me. "So what did John have to say when you told him?"

"He was upset of course, but he said he already knew she was having an affair."

Billy sat up straighter. "John already knew?"

I nodded. "Yeah, he said he suspected something when he found the birth control pills, so he followed her and saw them together."

After removing his arm from around me, he pulled a small notebook and a pen from his front pocket, and wrote down, "John knew Kasey was having affair." Then he looked at me. "You know this doesn't look good, Lorry. Kasey may or may not get off the hook, but this makes John a suspect, too. Which makes sense, really."

Billy and I had been to dinner at John and Kasey's house several times. And they had been here. One time, the six of us drove down to the valley to go to an amusement park in Phoenix. So Billy knew them well. And it was Billy's idea to hang out with them, because although she was my cousin, I had never associated with her that much. But Billy thought since Lily was Aiden's best friend, that we should allow them to play together as often as we could. And now this. It wasn't good for anybody.

"I never thought of that. It does look bad, doesn't it? Jilted husband kills wife's lover. Yeah, that's an easy conclusion to come to."

Billy stuffed the notebook and pen back in his pocket, settled back on the couch, and put his arm back around me. He pulled me close and kissed me on the temple. "Do you think John did it?"

"No, definitely not. Do you?"

He sat for a minute thinking before answering. "No, it doesn't seem like John's way. What exactly did he say to you about it?"

"He said that if Kasey really loved him, then she would come back to him. John showed no animosity at all, just sadness."

Sighing, Billy shook his head. "I better go question him tomorrow. I hate to put any more on the poor guy, with Kasey just coming home from jail—if she comes home—but I really have to."

"What do you mean *if she comes home* from jail? They'll give her bail, won't they? She's got two kids. So she wouldn't be a flight risk, would she?"

"It's not that, Lorry. It's that she tried to wipe her fingerprints off the gun. That's destruction of evidence in a felony. The prosecuting attorney is sure to make a big deal about that. Do you know if John got her a lawyer yet?"

"I don't know. We should get Bryan down here to defend her." Bryan O'Keefe was the man who came down immediately from Flagstaff to help me when Billy threw me into a holding cell after finding me with Eddie's dead body. Bryan was a good friend.

"Good idea. Why don't you call him and find out if he's available tomorrow morning? Then call John and tell him that you took care of it. Poor guy could use all the help he can get right now."

I walked into the kitchen, took the phone from its

cradle, and punched in Bryan's number. He was available, and he'd be happy to do it. I gave him the information and called John. Poor John had just given Zandor a bath and was putting him to bed. He had never even thought about getting an attorney for Kasey.

When I returned to Billy and told him what John had said, he shook his head. "He didn't even think to get her an attorney? Doesn't that sound kind of weird to you? Look at this scenario: he kills the wife's lover, and since he's still angry at the wife, he doesn't even get her an attorney. It sounds perfectly logical, doesn't it?"

"This is the scenario I see: heartbroken husband picks up infant from daycare, brings him home to an empty house, changes his diaper, feeds him, bathes him, rocks him to sleep. I think it more likely that he never thought of it. Having your wife in jail and needing an attorney isn't an everyday occurrence in most people's lives. Anyway, forget about John, what did the wife say?"

"She was just leaving when I got there. When I told her I needed to talk to her, she seemed nervous and said Derek already questioned her. I think Derek might have gotten suspicious and warned her I might be coming. But we went into the house and talked. She was cooperative."

"What did she say?"

"When I asked if she knew her husband was having an affair, she answered no *too quickly*."

"What do you mean 'too quickly'?"

"Like she had been told to say no. Derek would know that would make her look more guilty, and he probably coached her not to acknowledge that she knew. After I asked her a bunch more questions, I asked if she knew he was having the affair with the other woman. She

45

hesitated and then said she did know. Since I was sure that Derek wouldn't think of warning her about that—he might not even have known about the other girlfriend—I thought that was telling.

"When I asked her how she knew about the other girlfriend, she said 'a woman just knows.' Which makes me think she did know about Kasey. But there's no way to prove it. Besides, I didn't get the feeling that she did it. Not that I'm right all the time"—he smiled and pulled me toward him affectionately—"but I just don't think so."

What he was talking about is when he thought that I had killed Eddie. I didn't smile back. Memories of being in that ten-by-ten concrete holding cell still haunted me. Billy tried to make light of it, but it was something that maybe I still hadn't totally forgiven him for.

CHAPTER ELEVEN

AS I PREPARED breakfast for Aiden and Lily, I thought back on the conversation from the night before. After Billy's comment about not always being right and after he realized how I took the comment, he quickly changed the subject from murder to lighter subjects. The evening ended well, he kissed me good night and said he'd see me in court in the morning.

If Kasey did get bail—and hopefully, with Bryan at the helm, she would—but if she *did* get bail, Billy expected it to be a lot—more than John and Kasey's house was worth. So my second job in the morning after dropping the kids off at school, was to go to the bank and get several cashier's checks in varying denominations. I didn't want Kasey to have to stay in that nasty place one second longer than she had to.

Aiden, who knows I don't give him pancakes on school days, begged for them because they were Lily's favorite. How could I not give in? The kid was distraught. Lily had woken us all that morning with a scream and then had rushed into my room and thrown herself into my half-asleep arms.

"Nothing bad will happen to my mommy, will it, Aunt Lorry?" I wasn't her aunt and Kasey wasn't Aiden's aunt —we were all cousins—but the kids preferred to address us that way, and Kasey and I didn't care.

"No, honey, nothing bad will happen," I said with a confidence I didn't feel. "Bryan is going to help her out today, and then, hopefully, she can come home."

"Mommy's coming home today?" she asked.

"I hope so, Lily, I hope so."

She sat up, but the tears still dripped out of her eyes. "Then I don't want to go to school. I want to see Mommy!"

I pulled her back down and hugged her to me. By that time, Aiden had come in and snuggled up beside her. "Lily, honey, you will see your mommy when you get out of school today. Since I don't know when she'll get home, you can't be there alone to wait for her."

"I'll stay with you then."

That's all I needed was wild, distraught Lily with me at the historical society. "I'll be gone in the morning, and I don't know when I'll get back." It was the truth. I was going to Coyote Moon to bail her mother out of jail—*if* she got bail at all, which wasn't for sure yet.

Lily crossed her arms in front of her, which wasn't easy, since she was squeezed in between me and Aiden. "I don't want to go to school! I'm not going!"

"Lily, it won't be the same without you there. Who would I play with?" crooned Aiden. He always knew *exactly* the right thing to say. What would I do without that kid?

"Um, I really don't want to go," said Lily, but without as much fervor.

"Please, Lily, please. I'd really like to have you there

with me."

Lily sighed. "Okay, Aiden, I'll go for you." I could still see the tears sliding down her face. But I appreciated her loyalty to Aiden.

"Let's get up now and have breakfast!" I gave the kids a gentle push to encourage them off the bed, and when that didn't work, I climbed out the other side. After letting Bingo outside for his morning constitutional, I walked into the kitchen. It was there, when Lily was in the bathroom, that Aiden asked for the pancakes.

So I served them pancakes, and Lily, in her usual flamboyant fashion, spilled the sticky syrup all over the table. But I got it cleaned up, got the kids and me dressed, and headed off to drive them to school. Aiden and I usually walked from the historical society, but I had already told Aiden, while Lily was in the bathroom, that I didn't want to do that today.

Next, I made a quick trip to the bank to pick up the cashier's checks. I had already called from home to have the money wired into my account. But by that time, I was running late, and after getting caught in traffic on my way to Coyote Moon courthouse, I arrived late. I opened all the windows in the car an inch, parked in the shade, left water in the car, told Bingo to stay, and then ran for the courtroom.

The door to the courtroom was closed, and there was a sign with red letters on it that said *Caution: Automatic Door.* Carefully, I opened the door and walked into the back of the courtroom, still out of breath from running —as best as I could run with three-inch heels—from the parking lot, and Billy was sitting at the back waiting for me.

He stood up and whispered, "Where were you? It's

almost over."

"Between kids, money, and traffic, it's the best I could do." I looked around the courtroom. It was painted an off-white with a green tinge to it. Green, yellow, and beige noise panels adorned the room and the ceiling. The entryway had a red rug, then a strip of beige rug, but most of the room had a green rug. A wood-paneled barrier, topped with gray, separated the audience from the participants. To the left was the jury box; and the prosecutor's table, complete with a microphone, was closest to that. The defendant's table was on the right. Along with the prosecutor, sat Derek and Nick; and Bryan and Kasey sat at the defendant's table. She looked disheveled and like she had been crying.

The judge sat elevated above the proceedings and held his gavel in his hand. Behind him to the left was the American flag and to the right was the Arizona flag. Directly behind him was a plaque of the Arizona state seal with a date on the bottom: 1912.

Billy took my arm and pulled me to the chairs. I had expected benches, but apparently individual chairs were the latest courtroom accoutrements. He sat down and indicated me to sit beside him. The chair had metal legs and a plastic seat with a thin covering of upholstery cushion over it. There were gross-looking spots on my chair. I ran my fingers along it to make sure the spots weren't fresh, and then I sat down.

The judge pounded his gavel. "Bail is set at five hundred thousand dollars." Kasey gasped and the prosecutor nodded in triumph.

"Bryan did a great job. She almost didn't get bail at all," Billy whispered.

"Now what?"

"Bail has to be paid."

"Where do I go?"

"The jail."

CHAPTER TWELVE

BILLY SAID *THE jail*, but the official name of the place was the Coyote Moon Detention Center. I had been there before—not only to bail Eddie out once, but more recently when I came to visit Zack when he was in jail. That was the place where I first met Zack. If you can call it met since we only saw each other through computer monitors.

The room I walked into was tiny, with security cameras in each corner of the room, following my movements. It was an eerie sensation, and made me feel guilty, even though I was there for benevolent purposes.

I walked to the counter in front of what I figured was bullet-proof glass. There was a drawer that could be slid in and out between the reception person and me. The woman who came to the counter wore a white blouse and gray slacks with a black stripe down the sides. She didn't smile but instead pointed to the visitor sheet on a clipboard attached to the window with a narrow chain. Apparently, a previous occupant of the room had stolen the clipboard and had inspired the chain as a countermeasure against future theft. There was also a chain attached to a pen, but someone had taken the ink reservoir out of the ballpoint pen. One would think things were safe inside a jail, but apparently one would be wrong.

I held up the pen with the missing innards, and she opened the drawer on her side and pushed another pen toward me. "I want it back," she said in an authoritative voice.

Nodding, I signed my name quickly and dropped the pen back in the drawer. She took it out and asked, "What can I help you with?"

I remembered the sober expression on the last person I had dealt with in this room and concluded that the county hired people by their ability not to break into a smile. Apparently, people who paid bail and came to visit inmates did not want to be greeted with a smile. That's all that I could come up with. "I need to pay bail for someone, please."

She clicked the mouse on her computer and with her hands on the keyboard, said, "Name, please."

"Kasey Brannigan."

I saw her eyes get big when she saw the amount of the bail. "That will be five hundred thousand dollars."

Reaching into my purse, I pulled out the assortment of cashier's checks I had, picked out five hundred thousand, and put it into the sliding drawer. She pulled it out, examined it, held it up to the light, and put it into her cash drawer. Then she nodded and buzzed someone in the back. "Kasey Brannigan to be released," she said into the microphone. Turning to me, she said, "She'll be out here in a few minutes."

Fifteen minutes later, Kasey came dragging through the door, looking bedraggled and wearing her canary yellow waitress uniform from the Rutledge Koffee Korner Kafe—what she was wearing when they took her in. The woman behind the counter said, "Here are your belongings, Mrs. Brannigan." It was a plastic bag with a handful of change in it—her tips from the morning before Derek and Nick had dragged her off to jail.

"Keep it!" said Kasey and then she wrapped her arms around me and began to sob in that kind of way that gives you the hiccups and takes your breath away. Her tears were falling on my new blue blazer, and I hoped that tears didn't stain. It's not something I had ever considered before.

"Come on, Kasey, let's go to the car." I opened the door, helped her out—because it was like she could barely stand on her own—and we walked together in silence out to my light blue RAV4.

Silence was not a word that would normally be in the same sentence as Kasey. She was the most talkative person I had ever met. I used to say that she didn't have any periods or paragraphs—her conversations were all one big blur, subjects changed at random, and no pauses in between. If you needed her to be quiet, it was all you could do to find a place to say, "Stop!" So her uncharacteristic silence scared me.

When we got to the car, I walked her to the passenger door, unlocked it, and helped her inside. She fell into the seat like she had no strength left in her legs. I got into the driver's side, started the car, and looked at her. Kasey sat there with her hands over her face and tears sliding down her face. As soon as I stepped on the gas, she again broke out in those deep sobs that come from the gut. I patted her on the arm and kept driving toward her house.

When Bingo moved into the front seat from the back and licked her, she pushed him away. I always thought a dog's attention was a comforting thing, but apparently Kasey didn't feel the same way, so I told Bingo to get in the back and leave her alone.

CHAPTER THIRTEEN

AS WE DROVE, I decided to leave Kasey in her uncharacteristic silence and her tears. I looked at her at stoplights and patted her arm to let her know I was there for her. After fifteen minutes, she finally spoke.

"Oh, Lorry, it was horrible. From the moment they took me in to when I walked through that door when you picked me up."

"I saw that Derek adjusted the handcuffs too tight, but I was glad that Nick loosened them for you."

"Not just that, but when Derek buckled me into the seat belt, he touched my breasts—not with his hands, it was his forearm—but I could tell it was deliberate." She shook her head. "And then being questioned at the sheriff's station, and the fingerprints, and that horrible little room, and then being charged with murder and taken to jail in Coyote Moon. And that jail was awful, too. I think it was psychological, you know, 'I'm in jail!,' but it was more than that, too. It was wondering if they would really catch who did it and if I would ever be released, or if I would be stuck in prison and have all those horrible things happen to me like in prison movies." She shook her head slowly back and forth. "It was terrible. I hope I never have to go back there."

Without looking at her, I glanced sideways to see that tears were still running down her face. And then she asked the question that I was wondering if she would ask.

"Where's John? Why didn't he come to pick me up?"

"I called him last night to set up Bryan as your attorney, and he said nothing about it."

"Do you think he's angry at me?" she asked in a high-pitched voice.

I looked at her like she was nuts. "Kasey!" I said with more force than I intended. "How would you feel if you found out he was messing around on you?"

She shook her head again, quick this time. "Oh, John would never mess around on me. He's not that kind of man."

"And I didn't think *you* were that kind of woman."

"I can't talk about it, Lorry. I did what I did, and I'm sorry I hurt John, but I'm not sorry I did it. I needed to know I was still attractive to other men."

"You're talking about a midlife crisis, Kasey! You're only thirty-two! It's a little early."

"I got married when I was eighteen. It's not too early." When she said it like that, it sounded logical. And then she was silent again until we pulled up in front of her house.

"Kasey, I'd be happy to keep Lily with me tonight so you have a chance to—you know—be alone with John and talk."

She turned toward me with a grim look on her face. "My daughter Lily needs to know I'm home and I'm okay. I want her home with me. But I would appreciate it if you could pick her up for me and drop her off here. John and I will have plenty of time to talk after she goes to bed."

"All right, Kasey, I'd be happy to bring her home for you. Be sure to call Pamela to let her know that it's okay for me to pick her up."

"I know you think I'm an airhead, Lorry, and maybe I am, but I can take care of my own daughter. Of course I'll call Pamela." Kasey got out of the car and slammed the door. She walked a few paces, turned back, and knocked on the window until I pushed the button to lower it.

"Lorry, I know you're judging me for this, and I'm asking you not to. I never judged you for your relationship with Eddie even though everyone but you knew he was wrong for you. We all knew how he abused you, and how he messed around on you, and how he was with you for your money. I never judged you. So, please, Lorry, *don't* judge me."

Without saying another word, she turned and walked away. I sat there appalled and ashamed. Then I waited until she stepped into the house before I drove away. Instead of driving back to work, I drove past the high school to a place by the river we used to park as kids. It wasn't a parking spot as in necking, it was a parking spot to listen to the river and think. Although I'm sure there was some necking going on as well, but not for me.

I didn't go there to throw myself in the river for my bad behavior, although it might have crossed my mind. Rolling down the window, I cranked the heat in the car, put the seat warmer on, and sat there listening to the river. Closing my eyes, I just listened and tried not to think of everything that Kasey had said to me. Not only had her words hurt me, they had shamed me. And I deserved every word. I felt the shame in every fiber of my being.

Something else bothered me about what she had said: that Eddie was with me for my money. *Every*one knew that except me? How stupid could I have been? Although it wasn't just that I was stupid, it's that I was, well, not exactly desperate, but somewhat desperate. Eddie may have pretended to love me—now I'll never know if it was real or not, even a little—but he was the only one who ever even bothered to pretend. Everyone needs to feel loved. In his own despicable way, he made me feel loved—not often, but more often than anyone else ever had. How sad is that?

CHAPTER FOURTEEN

BEFORE I STARTED the car to drive back to the society, I thought about something else. When Billy and I first started "dating," if you could call it that, because it happened quickly that we became *a couple*, but when it began, and because of my experience with Eddie, I wondered if he was getting involved with me for my money. Because that was right after I had come into possession of all my mother's millions.

When I finally worked up enough courage to broach the subject with him, he looked at me, nodded his head, but didn't say a word. He squeezed my hands and said, "How about if you and Aiden come over for dinner tomorrow night?"

We had been together for more than a month at that point, and I had never been to his house. And although I thought that was strange, he was a bachelor after all, and I thought maybe he was just a slob and didn't want me over there. I said yes to dinner, and he said he'd pick us up. When I argued that I could drive, he said it would be better if he picked us up.

As we drove, he turned onto Hillside Terrace—the

most exclusive street in Rutledge *and* the street where I grew up. In a mansion, I might add. The Lockharte Mansion. So it shocked me when he turned down that street. As we drove by the Lockharte Mansion, Billy pointed it out to Aiden. "That is where your mommy grew up, Aiden."

Aiden said, "Wow! That's huge, Mom! Can we live there again?"

"No, sweetie. I like where we live now." And then I turned to Billy and said, "You knew? I didn't realize that you knew."

He laughed. "Of course I knew! The Lockhartes are *legend* around here!"

We got to the end of the block, a cul-de-sac, and there stood one of the smaller houses on the block, freshly painted, and the yard in the process of new landscaping. Billy was doing all the work himself. He had bought the house as a fixer-upper and was enjoying making it into his home. But any house on that street—Hillside Terrace —was beaucoup bucks. He parked in front of the house and turned to me.

"Lorry, I never showed you before because I didn't want you to like me because of *my* money."

It turned out that Billy had a ton of money, too. His father had made several really smart investments. He and I were both richer than we ought to be. And his house wasn't sloppy at all—but many of the rooms were still in a shambles because he was remodeling them.

Aiden and I got out of the car, and Billy put his arms around both of us. "I guess neither of us have to worry that the other is after us because of our money." And then he kissed me.

That was another time that I felt ashamed—thinking

that about Billy when I was so wrong. But how could I not think that when the pain and hurt from Eddie was still so fresh?

Parked in front of the river, I took a deep breath, tried to forgive myself, and then considered slapping my face for punishment for being such a despicable person to Kasey. In my defense, I thought she was too much of an airhead to even notice. Wait. That makes me sound even worse, doesn't it? Taking another deep breath, I finally decided that I should just give it up and drive back to work.

I parked in the back and walked into the building. Petra, buried in her computer monitor, didn't even notice me standing beside her desk. "Hey, Petra. I'm back. Thanks so much for taking care of the place."

She turned toward me. "Oh, no worries, Lorry. No one came in, and the phone never rang. You didn't miss a thing!" Having concluded the conversation and completely immersed in her studies, she turned back to her computer and tapped on the keys, summarily dismissing me.

I walked to my desk, plopped down in my chair, put my purse into the bottom drawer, and turned toward the fish tank behind my desk. Fish and their smooth movements had always been relaxing for me. Well, that's not true. Not always. When I was with Eddie, he hated my fish and convinced me that I hated them too.

But once I left him, I learned the error of my ways, thanks to Petra. She had pointed out how many ways I had become who Eddie was instead of my own person. I had adopted *his* poor attitudes and beliefs. It took me awhile to get back to who I really was. I wasn't even sure who that was. That happens sometimes when one is with an abusive partner. Their life and their beliefs become one's own. I was so glad I was away from that kind of behavior. Billy was nothing like that, and *that* made me happy.

And as I thought that, Billy pulled his patrol car up in front of the historical society and walked in, setting the bell a-jingling. Standing up, I wrapped my arms around him and buried my head in his chest. I held on as tight as I could.

"What's this about?" He hugged me as tight as I hugged him. Billy always knew what I needed.

After one last squeeze, I pulled away from him and sat down. I tightened my lips and said, "I'll tell you later. What's up?"

"I just interviewed John."

"And? What did he say?"

"Not much more than he told you. He confirmed that he *did* know she was fooling around, but he never considered doing anything about it. He has no alibi except that he was home with Kasey until she left. So they are each other's alibis—which isn't good enough— but I have to keep digging. Unless they did it together, which would be unlikely, I don't think either of them did it. But who did?"

"That's the question of the hour, isn't it?"

Billy frowned and put his hand on my shoulder. "Listen, I have to drive to the valley tomorrow. I'll be gone most of the day."

"What are ya doin'?"

"Going to see Charles Jones's girlfriend."

"Charles Jones?" I asked, and then it occurred to me. "Oh! The dead guy!"

Billy cleared his throat. He didn't like it when I was

disrespectful of the dead. "Um, yes. The deceased."

"I want to go!" Jumping up, I ran into Petra's office. "Petra, would you mind holding down the fort tomorrow? I have to go to the valley with Billy!"

Petra, without looking up, waved her hand at me. "Yeah, sure, just leave me alone now."

I started walking back to Billy and then remembered something else. "Oh, and I need to pick up Lily, but I'll just drop her off and then come right back. Okay?"

She waved her hand again. "Whatever."

That was my line, and she stole it. I was teaching her bad habits.

When I walked back into my office, Billy said, "Lorry, I didn't say you could go with me. It's inappropriate."

"I'll be your associate. It will be fine."

"What do you want to go for, anyway?"

"To *feel* what it feels like in her house. You can tell a lot about a person that way. I want to see if she did it."

"That's why *I'm* going down to question her."

"And that's why I should go."

Billy shook his head in defeat. "Why are you picking up Lily? Is she staying with you again?"

"No, Kasey asked me to pick her up and drop her off."

"Did you offer to keep her another night so she and John would have time to talk?"

"Of course. And Kasey said she needed Lily to know that her mother was home and safe. And Kasey also said she and John would have plenty of time to talk."

"Sounds like she doesn't want to have that conversation."

"That's exactly what I was thinking."

"All right. So I can come over for dinner the usual

64

time, then?"

"Sure. Noodle Knoodle?"

"Great idea." He leaned over and gave me a peck on the lips. "And we'll talk about the valley then."

"I want to go, Billy."

"I know you do. We'll see."

I stuck my lips out like I was pouting, and he leaned over again and kissed them. "See ya later." And he stepped out the door.

CHAPTER FIFTEEN

WHEN IT WAS time, I drove to school to pick up Lily and Aiden. They were standing at the top of the stairs when I arrived. Aiden had his arm around Lily, but she didn't look like she was crying. They started walking toward the car, and Lily crossed her arms over her chest and looked defiant. I stepped out of the car and walked around it. Lily got to me, looked up with an unhappy face, and said, "I want to go home! I'm not going to your house! I want to go home!"

Although I tried to pull her to me in a hug, she stood her ground. Opening my arms toward her, I said, "Lily, I'm taking you home. Okay?"

She stayed rooted to the spot and moved her body left and right. "I don't believe you! You're just trying to trick me into coming to your house. I want to go home!"

Softly, I said, "Lily, have I ever lied to you before?"

Aiden spoke up then. He loved Lily but didn't like anyone calling his mother a liar. "My mommy is not a liar, Lily! If she says she will take you home, then she will!"

Lily looked from me to Aiden and back. "You

promise?"

I stood up straight and held my three fingers up in a Girl Scout salute. "I promise!"

Lily broke down then and threw herself in my arms. "Thank you, Aunt Lorry. Thank you."

"Come on. Get in the car. Your mommy is eager to see you."

"My mommy is home?"

I opened the door of the car, and the two kids climbed inside. "Yes, she's waiting. Put your seat belts on and let's go."

Pulling up in front of Kasey's house, I noticed that she was standing right outside the door. She never looked at me, just kept her eyes on Lily, who opened the back door and ran to her mother without closing the door. Kasey knelt down and they hugged, and I could tell by the slight jerks of their bodies that they were both crying. Without so much as a wave or a glance at me, Kasey stood up and ushered Lily inside.

"Is Aunt Kasey mad at us?" Aiden asked after he pulled the back door of the car closed. "She didn't wave to us or anything."

"I think Kasey has a lot on her mind right now, Aiden. And she was really glad to see Lily."

Aiden cuddled Bingo, who was on his lap, and said nothing else while we drove back to the historical society. I parked in the back, and then the three of us walked inside.

"Hey, Petra. Was it busy?"

She was faced toward her monitor, so Aiden put his arms around her from behind. "Hi there, kiddo. No, not at all. One person came in, walked through the exhibit area briefly, bought one postcard and left. No biggie."

When I started walking into my office area, Petra called me back. She turned to look at me. "Listen, Martha called and asked me to help you with this, but honestly, I think you can handle it yourself. Every year, we add a new exhibit—you know, to freshen things up a bit—and to get people in town to come take a look. Would you mind doing it on your own? If you need any help or advice, I'll be here, of course."

Martha was our boss who worked at the Town Offices. She was the one who hired me, let me stay at her bed and breakfast when I didn't have anywhere else to go, and who, with her husband Hugo, were like grandparents to Aiden. I loved Martha.

"Yes, yes, I can do it myself. Anything, Petra. I just really appreciate you covering for me when I'm gone. I know how important your school work is to you." I was grateful that I could do something for Petra with all the times she'd been covering for me lately. And it didn't sound like a big deal anyway.

Aiden jumped up and down. "I can help too! I can help!"

I hugged him, and we walked together into my office. "We can handle it, Petra. Not to worry!"

There was a messenger envelope on my desk from Martha, so after I got settled in, I opened it. Inside were some papers to be typed, and also a note from Martha about the exhibit project that Petra had just told us about. Martha wanted the new exhibit finished by the first of the year which meant we had a little over a month. It was almost Thanksgiving, so most of that week would be shot. We needed to start working on it as soon as we could.

Aiden grabbed my hand and pulled me toward the

back. "Come on, Mom! Let's get started!"

As we passed Petra's desk, I asked, "How are we going to add any? It's already full back there."

"Pick one to get rid of. And when you put it back upstairs, leave a note on it to say when it was last used."

"Makes sense," I commented, but Petra couldn't hear me. "Let's start at the first one, Aiden."

We walked together to the first exhibit which was the old-time school exhibit with the old desks, the blackboard, and a picture of the old one-room schoolhouse. "I like this one. I don't think we should replace it," said Aiden.

"Agreed."

So we moved on to the next one which was clothes from the nineteenth century including the ever-famous and most popular little boy wearing a skirt. "This one is too popular."

"Agreed."

The next one was the exhibit for Grizelda's Bar, which had been in existence for more than a hundred years. And still was, although it had gone through a few changes. "How 'bout this one, Mom?"

"Of course you would think this one!" I ruffled his hair. "Let's keep it in mind and look at the rest."

Across the back was a double exhibit with old-time pictures of birds on one side and old-time pictures of animals drinking from the same spot on the river on the other side. An old camera, alleged to be the one that took the pictures, separated the two sides. The pictures were all sepia-toned, but they were gorgeous. Rutledge was in an interesting place geographically—close to colder Flagstaff to the north and close to more desert-y Sedona on the east. So we got a large variety of birds, and the display showed a ton of them. And the animals at the river—before the river was polluted, that is—showed javelina, deer, coyote, fox, and pronghorn antelope, which as you probably know are not antelope at all. But they were pretty, and they were in the display, too. "I like this one, Mom. We should leave it."

"I like it, too, Aiden."

"This one's my favorite!" Aiden pointed to another double exhibit displaying the railroad that used to go through the mountains between Sedona and Rutledge. Originally, it had been destined to hook up with the Verde Canyon Railroad, but since the trains kept falling off the track, they had to nix that idea. The Verde Canyon Railroad had more luck and was still in existence. The display had a picture that someone caught of the train going over the bank, and it also had a hobby-sized engine that was just like the original, and then another hobby-sized diorama of the train lying at the bottom of the ravine upside down.

"Okay, then! Moving on!"

Rocks and minerals of Rutledge were showcased in the next exhibit. The coolest thing about this exhibit, I thought, was the slice of a petrified tree, complete with tree rings. It was beautiful and unexpected. "Not this one, Mom. I like rocks and minerals. And isn't that petrified tree cool?"

"That's my favorite part, too, Aiden! You know, we're running out of possibilities here."

"There's always Grizelda's Bar," said Aiden.

"Let's see what else we've got before we decide."

We stopped in front of the exhibit that showed a bunch of old machines, including an old typewriter with the round keys and the carriage return, an old telephone in a box with a crank, an old adding machine with ones on the bottom, twos next, then threes, and even an old sewing machine that showed the treadle.

"This is pretty cool," said Aiden.

"Agreed."

"It's either the next one or Grizelda's, Mom." Aiden looked up at me with a crooked smile.

We both moved in front of the next exhibit, called Seasons of Rutledge. It showed beautiful color, nine-by-twelve pictures of the different seasons in Rutledge.

"It's this one, Mom."

"Yup, I agree. It's this one."

"Now we get to go upstairs and find a new one!" Aiden ran up the stairs.

"You check 'em out. I need to finish some typing. I'll be up in a while."

"Nope," said Petra, as she walked down the hall toward me. "Time to go home now!"

CHAPTER SIXTEEN

WE DROVE HOME, and although I knew I should start dinner so it would be ready when Billy arrived, I just couldn't. It had been a difficult, emotional day. I plopped down on the couch and just sat there, not even a book in my hands.

Aiden noticed. "Mom? You're not sick are you?"

I motioned for him to sit with me. He curled right up on my lap. Bingo tried to share, but even with my big lap, there was no room, so he had to content himself to sit beside us. "No, I'm not sick, but I am tired. It's been a trying day."

"Because of Aunt Kasey?"

"Yeah."

"Maybe we could have pizza tonight!" Aiden was always ready for pizza.

"We had it last night, Aiden."

"So? I still love it!"

I hugged him to me. "I know you do, kiddo, and so do I, but not every night."

Then the phone in the kitchen rang, so I boosted Aiden off my lap and got up to answer it. "Hello? . . .

Hi, Billy. . . . No, I haven't started yet. . . . Really? Yeah! . . . Okay, see ya soon. . . . And thanks! . . . Love you, too. Bye." I was so happy that I jumped and when I came down, I almost broke my high heel and bent my ankle. But I didn't, and that made me even happier. "Billy is going to bring Chinese takeout for dinner tonight! Yippee!"

Aiden ran into the kitchen and jumped into my waiting arms. I swung him around as Bingo barked at my feet. After I put Aiden down, I walked to my room to change clothes.

Aiden followed me. "Sheriff Billy is sure a nice guy, isn't he, Mom?"

"Yes, he is, Aiden. I agree." And I closed the door to my room, and Aiden said nothing more.

When I came out again a few minutes later, Billy had already arrived and put the food onto the table. We had done this many times, and Billy had it down pat. Vegetarian spring rolls and egg drop soup for Aiden, and egg rolls and wonton soup for me and Billy. For the main dish, Aiden liked chicken chow mein, and Billy and I shared kung pao chicken and sweet and sour pork. When Aiden couldn't eat all his chow mein, Billy and I finished it off for him. This was the usual procedure and left all of us stuffed to the gills.

After dinner, we played Uncle Wiggly and Chutes and Ladders. They were both too easy for Aiden, but he liked them. And Billy and I both enjoyed Chutes and Ladders. At the end of the evening, Billy put Aiden to bed and read to him while I watched at the door—so I wouldn't miss any of the story!

After he turned out the light, Billy came out of Aiden's room, put his arm around me, and headed toward the front door. When I saw where he was leading me, I stopped short and put my hands on my hips.

"Wait a minute, buster! You're not going to get away with us not talking about tomorrow!"

Billy smiled, pulled me to him, and kissed me soundly on the mouth. "I'll pick you up at 9:30 at the historical society." Then he disappeared out the door, but not before locking the deadbolt from the outside. He knew I sometimes forgot, and he was still concerned after what had happened a few months earlier when someone had sneaked into the back door and—oh, I don't even like to think about it.

It had been a fun and relaxing evening, but the emotional events of the day had taken their toll. I felt tired but way too wired to sleep, and too tired to read. So I sunk onto the couch, put my head back, and started thinking.

Why had I been so eager to go to the valley with Billy? I guess because it bothered me that the ex-girlfriend had called Chuck Jones this week and then he had wound up dead. What did she call him about? I wondered why Kasey hadn't told me that or even if she knew. Maybe she didn't. That would be something to pursue. Kasey had certainly told Billy about that. Hadn't she? That still didn't explain my enthusiasm to accompany Billy down to the valley.

There was something there I couldn't get my head around. I went over the possible suspects: Zack, who wasn't a suspect at all; Kasey, who I would reluctantly have to admit was not a suspect, either; John, Kasey's husband, who I didn't think in a million years would murder anyone—but I didn't think in a million years that Kasey would mess around on him, either, so maybe he should still be considered; Chuck Jones's wife, who I did consider a real possibility; and Chuck Jones's previous girlfriend, *who called him this week*. That, to me, was the most telling. And I, you know, just had a *feeling* about her. That's why I had to go to the valley with Billy. Something was still nagging at me like I should include someone else, but I was finally getting tired enough to sleep, so I let it slip out of my mind.

CHAPTER SEVENTEEN

THE FOLLOWING MORNING as we ate breakfast together, Aiden eating cereal and toast, and me eating a soft-boiled egg, we talked about the day. Aiden wore his Winnie the Pooh feet pajamas, and I wore a flannel nightgown.

"Can I go?" he asked.

"You have school."

"Yes, but I'm ahead of everybody in the class. It won't hurt my grades."

"It's police business, Aiden."

"Sheriff's business, you mean. But if it's sheriff's business, then you shouldn't be going, either." The kid was too smart for his own good and definitely too smart for my good.

"That may be true, but I managed to convince Billy that I should go to keep him company and to assist in the investigation."

Aiden smiled and nodded his head. "You know who did it?"

Shrugging, I said, "I have a feeling."

"Feelings are good," he said, "but facts are better."

"Have you been talking to Billy about law enforcement again?" And then we both laughed.

A half hour later after me cleaning up the kitchen and fixing Aiden's lunch, and both of us getting dressed, we left. I parked at the back of the historical society like I usually did and walked Aiden to school as I always did. When I returned to the historical society and walked down the hallway, I saw that Petra was already there.

"Hey, Petra."

"Hey."

"Listen, if Billy and I get hung up down there, can you babysit Aiden tonight?"

"Can't promise a thing, Lorry, because it depends on how many people come in today. If it's like yesterday, then I probably can. If it gets busy in here and I can't get any of my schoolwork done, then I will have to study tonight at the library."

"Well, that's okay then. Martha and Hugo can probably do it. It's all right, though, isn't it, if Aiden comes here after school like usual?"

"Yeah, that's fine. Bye, now."

That was Petra's way of saying that the conversation was over, and she needed to get back to work. I patted her on the shoulder and walked into my office.

It was good that Billy wasn't picking me up until 9:30. I wanted to type the papers I had received from Martha the day before. Taking them from my desk, I carefully proofed them. They were both short; that was good. In fifteen minutes, I was finished—which was also good, because I saw Billy's patrol car pull up in front. Quickly, I attached them to an email and sent them along to Martha.

"Petra? I'm leaving with Billy now. Thanks for taking

care of Aiden this afternoon, and if we're late, I'll call and let you know who will take care of him this evening. Thanks for everything. See ya!"

"Bye" is all she said.

I hopped out the door, across the sidewalk, and then hopped into Billy's car. "Hey, Billy," I said as I leaned over to kiss him. Then I belted myself in and looked around the car. Although I had sat in the back seat of his patrol car several months ago, I had never been in the front seat before.

First thing I did was snoop: I opened the glove compartment. I expected a gun or taser or something exciting, but unfortunately, there was only the owner's manual for the car. It wasn't really a car, though, it was officially an SUV. The outside of it was white with a horizontal black stripe running from the back door all the way up to just this side of the headlight. And on the front door, there was a gold sheriff's star overlaid on top of the black stripe.

I felt cramped. There was a big computer monitor to the left of me. The keyboard was to Billy's right. "Can we move this thing? Put it in the back or something?"

"Of course, we can't! It's built in and I need it!"

"All right," I grumbled.

"Don't make me sorry I brought you, Lorry," he said more petulantly than I'm sure he felt.

"I wouldn't do that, sweetie." I leaned over and kissed him on his shoulder. Then I went back to grumbling. "Can you explain these things to me?"

Billy went on a long, exaggerated explanation of everything I could see and that he could point to while he was driving. The gist of it was there was a GPS and a radar gun mounted on the upper window of the driver's side. The rearview mirror had a display of the radar gun's target area. On the console between us was a flashlight, a small armrest for the driver, a public announcement system with its own microphone, and what he called a Code Three panel. Basically Code Three was "use lights and siren."

The first thing he pointed to on the panel was the gun release to unlock the rifle. "A rifle?" I asked. "You have a rifle in here?"

"Of course," he replied calmly. "All cop cars are equipped with a rifle. This one is locked, and you unlock it here." Billy pointed to the button on the panel.

"Where's the rifle?" I looked at him and in front of me and didn't see it anywhere.

"Right here." He used his right thumb to point to a rifle that was standing up between the seats, behind my left shoulder. I don't know why I didn't notice it when I stepped into the car—it was probably that the console was so intriguing.

"Oh! Okay." It just shocked me that it was in the car with us—it didn't scare me or anything. After all, I was with Billy. While I was looking at the rifle, I noticed the partition between the front seat and back seat, which was designed to keep the criminal element away from the officers. Behind the driver, the partition was made of glass, and behind the passenger side was a heavy metal screen-like material.

Then Billy finished explaining the Code Three panel, which included the light bar and siren, spotlight, different settings for the light bar, and an airhorn. The light bar on top could be an arrow to guide people around an accident. I thought that was cool. It sounded useful, but I didn't think I'd ever seen it used before—not that much ever happened in Rutledge. You know, except murder.

Billy said, "Usually, we get to an accident and our lights are blazing, and by the time things settle down, we forget that we could have used it. But in case we ever remember, it's available!" Billy laughed, a light, easy laugh that I was now used to with him. He glanced quickly at me, and his eyes sparkled. I do love that man.

"So what's the plan?" I looked out the window and saw that the wind was blowing hard. "It's awful windy out there."

"It will be fine, Lorry. I thought we could take it easy and drive through Jerome on our way, and then head down to the valley."

"Jerome?"

"Yeah. Have you been there?"

"Yeah. But I didn't think we'd be going today."

Billy shrugged. "I thought it would be a pleasant diversion. We won't stop. But there are some awesome views coming down the mountain from up there."

"All right." I put my hand on his shoulder. "Any time I'm with you, it's a good time!"

After driving west through Coyote Moon to the two-lane highway going south, we took that to Cottonwood, and headed up the mountain on 89A. That side of the mountain wasn't too bad, but the other side was a twisty-turny road with a great view—and a big drop-off. But Billy was a good driver, and I wasn't going to worry about it.

Jerome used to be a booming copper mining town, but was now filled with art galleries and quaint little shops with photographs of the good ole days on the walls. They had an interesting historical society there, too.

Aiden and I had driven up there once to look at it and have lunch in town.

The bulk of the town was on two main streets and a hair-pin turn. To get from the one street to the other on foot required walking up or down a steep staircase. They had several. It was a pleasant place with a good atmosphere.

Billy made the turn, drove up slowly past the old buildings, and then we started down the mountain. I had heard that recently a car had gone over and fallen into the canyon below. The driver, stuck in the car, was only found because a tourist stopped by one of the scenic viewpoints, looked over the rail, and saw the car below. Now is that just dumb luck or is that *meant to be*? There's no question in my mind. But I didn't want to think about that lonely car lying upside down in the bottom of the canyon as Billy pointed his car downhill for our trip down Mingus Mountain.

CHAPTER EIGHTEEN

THE DRIVE DOWN the mountain wasn't bad, and the views were spectacular. But I have to admit that I was glad to get on flat ground again when we got to the bottom. And I noticed that the wind was still blowing hard. Clouds raced across the sky. We hadn't had rain in a couple of months. We needed the moisture, but monsoon season was over.

"You hungry?" Billy asked.

"I could probably eat," I said as I looked around. I could always eat. We were at the edge of Prescott Valley.

"I'm starved!" Billy said. "I didn't eat breakfast this morning. How 'bout Olive Garden? I could use some pasta about now, and their salads and breadsticks—"

"Say no more!"

The Olive Garden in Prescott was at the other end of a Walmart parking lot right on Highway 69. Looking up, it appeared that they had cut off half of a mountain or a big hill to build the complex which included—besides the Olive Garden—In and Out Burger and a US Bank. The half of the big hill showing from the parking lot was layered with two obvious horizontal cuts. A third of the way up from the bottom, several wimpy bushes had been planted on the narrow strip. A third of the way down from the top, the strip was just there with nothing to show for it. The half hill looked like the kind of situation that would have a bad ending with a heavy rain storm, because it didn't look like there was anything holding up the scarred hill.

When we got out of the car, there was the strong fragrance of soup in the air. It smelled good. We walked to the door, Billy opened it for me, and we walked inside.

There was an oversized wooden podium in front, and as we waited for someone to seat us, I glanced around the spacious restaurant. Directly behind the podium was a planter with some purple flowers in it. They looked real. There was a bar straight ahead with clean, sparkling glasses hanging down from a rack on the ceiling. Two couches, one on the front wall and one on the side wall, looked comfortable. To the left of the podium on the wall, there was a large picture of a tree. On either side of it were wall indentations with a vase of flowers in each. One had yellow flowers, the other red. They were either fake or needed water—or something.

To the right were several tables against the wall, which was that kind of stone where the pieces fit together in an attractive manner. At the first table, an older woman sat with her mother. In people-watching mode, I saw her grab a handful of salad and put it on her plate. Then she put the big bowl, with some salad left in it, on the seat beside her. What? There was plenty of room on the table. What was she going to do—stick some in her purse, salad dressing and all? When the waitress brought another big bowl of salad, the woman took the bowl and dumped the new salad into the bowl that was beside her on the seat.

The hostess, a tall, thin woman wearing black with a name tag on that said Tina, came to seat us then, and I was grateful that she seated us on the other side of the restaurant so I wouldn't have to watch any more of the sideshow. I wondered, though, if that woman would ultimately put that salad in her purse. Inquiring minds want to know. Gross.

Billy ordered tortellinis, and I ordered shells with marinara sauce. Several years ago, I had stopped getting spaghetti after the time one of the noodles somehow popped upward and left a mark of tomato sauce from my upper lip all the way to my forehead. That wouldn't have been so bad—I could have just wiped it off with my napkin—but the noodle had made a side trip to my left eye and gotten tomato sauce in it. I had to run to the bathroom and wash my eye out. I'd like to say I've never had spaghetti since, but there has been a time or two at friends' houses that they would serve spaghetti, and I wouldn't have a choice but to eat it. I would use my fork, though, to cut it up in tiny pieces. Tomato sauce is caustic, isn't it? I could have lost an eye!

Our salad and breadsticks came, and by the time we had eaten two orders of each, we barely had room for our meal. But somehow we stuffed it in and left there ready to take a nap. Both of us waddled out to the car, and we still had a lot of driving to do. I was glad that Billy was the one driving.

The drive down to the valley didn't seem so long, but maybe that was because when Billy accused me of falling asleep, I ignored it. Although I denied it, it was probably true. It made for a short ride, though!

"Where does she live?"

"Scottsdale."

"Ooooh. The rich part of town, huh?" Scottsdale was an affluent area just east of Phoenix. "What's her name?"

"Amanda Fletcher. Her husband is William Fletcher."

"Of the *Fletcher* Building?" I asked incredulously. The Fletcher Building was a huge office building built just outside of downtown Phoenix. It was one of the most exclusive buildings in town to have an office, and one of the most expensive. Rumor had it that their wait list was in the triple figures.

Billy nodded without looking at me. "Yup."

"And she's messing around on him?"

"No one knows their story, Lorry. Don't judge."

Chuckling under my breath, I just nodded. I had asked Billy to help me get over my judgmental-ness, and he had willingly obliged. Sometimes it was too much, but I had to admit that I had asked him.

Billy exited Interstate 17 and turned onto the Carefree Highway going east. Then a couple of more turns on streets I didn't recognize until we were driving south on Cave Creek Road. Billy's car followed the turns in the road, as the landscape entranced me with its stark beauty. Besides the McDowell Mountains, there was an abundance of saguaro cactus here, which I have to admit that I love. It must be all those cowboy movies I watched as a kid.

Unexpectedly—mainly because I was so immersed in the landscape—Billy turned into a long driveway lined on each side with more majestic saguaro cactus. Very impressive, but I hadn't seen the house yet. Okay, the house. First let me say that I grew up in a mansion, so I don't get impressed easily over big houses. This wasn't a big house. This wasn't even a mansion. This was a small city.

Several buildings surrounding a broad courtyard that had a fountain with a stone dolphin in the middle. One of the buildings was a four-car garage that looked like it had living quarters above it—probably the slave quarters —oops, I mean the servant quarters.

Billy parked in front of the main building and said, "Look, Lorry. I'm going to ask to go to the bathroom when we first get in there, so I can look around. You keep her busy chitchatting. Don't ask any questions yet, that will come later. When I get back, then you ask to go, and you look around. We'll compare notes after the interview. Clear?"

I raised my right hand in a saluting gesture. "Absolutely, Captain!"

CHAPTER NINETEEN

"AND I CAN'T open the door for you right now, because you're my associate, not my girlfriend. Okay?" he asked as he stepped out of the car. Billy was a chivalrous kind of guy, and I'm not embarrassed to say that I liked that.

The house was incredibly elegant, and if its insides looked anything like its outside, it would be spectacular indeed. The lush landscaping surrounding the compound was amazing. A variety of cactus and native grasses adorned the huge yard. Everything was in its place but made to look totally natural. And it achieved the look.

Billy rang the doorbell, which gave off a fancy multi-belled sound reminiscent of church bells, and after a several minute wait, a young man came to the door. I was expecting a butler, dressed in black and white and sporting a British accent, but this was a twenty-five-year-old man dressed in a sweatsuit. If I had to make a guess, I would guess that he was William Fletcher's son from a previous marriage.

"Yeah! Can I help you?" Then he glanced at Billy's

patrol car out front and raised his eyebrows.

"Yes. I'd like to see Amanda Fletcher, please." He pulled out his billfold and showed the man his identification card. "Rutledge Sheriff's Department."

The man opened the door, invited us in, and said, "I'll go get her. Wait here."

Directly in front of us was a massive grand staircase that looked like it was straight out of *Gone with the Wind*. To our right was a massive room with a huge sandstone fireplace in the center. Why you would need a fireplace in the valley was anybody's guess, but I wasn't judging. Believe me, I wasn't judging. To the left of us was a formal dining room with a mahogany table that would easily seat ten people.

Then we heard voices, and the man returned. "She'll be out in a minute." Then he walked away through the dining room into one of the two doors at the far end of the room.

"Weren't you going to ask to use the bathroom?" I whispered to Billy.

"Not until I introduce myself to her," he whispered back.

And she appeared. Mrs. William Fletcher. Amanda Fletcher. She looked no older than the man who answered the door. Tall and slim, she looked like a model. With her black hair and darker than night eyes that were slightly slanted, she looked foreign. And gorgeous. No wonder sixty-five-year-old William Fletcher would want her by his side. Arm candy. Trophy wife. If she was the killer, he would still pay top dollar for the most expensive lawyer in town. Was that being judgmental? Pardon me if I don't get over it in a week.

Amanda looked puzzled. "Yes? Can I help you?" She

was dressed in a purple terrycloth robe, and her hair was dripping wet. She looked like she had just come in from swimming. A mansion like this would certainly have a pool.

Billy showed her his identification card. "Billy Madrigal, ma'am, from the Rutledge Sheriff's Department. This is my associate, Lorry Lockharte." He motioned toward me, and I smiled at her. "I'd like to ask you a few questions, please." I wondered why he didn't say "we" but let it go.

She shrugged her shoulders. "Sure. Come on in here." Amanda walked toward the huge fireplace.

"Oh, Mrs. Fletcher, can I use your restroom? It's been a long drive down here."

She pointed toward the dining room. "See those two doors at the other side of the dining room? It's the one to the right. The other one leads to the kitchen."

"Thank you." Billy tilted his hat at her and walked in the direction she pointed.

"You have a beautiful home," I said.

Amanda smiled. "Come look at this view! I've always loved it!" She was proud of this house, and she should be. What a catch she made.

Leading the way past the huge but useless fireplace, she walked to the other end of the room and veered left. The room, connected to the bigger room with the fireplace, was all window on one side, and mostly window on the other side. She pointed out the bigger window.

"Look at that. I never tire of seeing it."

It was McDowell Mountain and was a lovely sight. And the beautiful desert with the saguaros leading up to it. "Yes, it is beautiful."

The window on the other side was to another room in the big house. An indoor pool with an underwater passage to the outdoor portion of the enormous pool. The oversized pool had an island in the middle with what looked like a hot tub. How unique that was! But the indoor portion of the pool also had a hot tub in one corner. More beautiful landscaping surrounded the outside pool including fountains and waterfalls.

"Incredible place you have, Mrs. Fletcher. The pool is awesome!"

"Oh, call me Amanda! I'm not into that social graces stuff!" She broadened her smile at me. "Yeah, I was swimming when you guys arrived."

Despite me thinking she was the killer, I had to like her. She actually seemed likable. But killers can do that, can't they? Charm you before they kill you?

Then Billy walked into the room. "Thank you, Mrs. Fletcher." I noticed that she didn't tell Billy not to call her that.

"Amanda, can I use that restroom, too? It was a long drive down here from Rutledge."

"Oh, yeah, sure. It's thataway." She smiled and pointed the direction Billy had come from. Amanda was so pleasant! How could she be a murderer?

I walked back by the fireplace, no comment, and into the dining room. Looking over my shoulder, I saw that since the room had curved right, she couldn't see me from there. Why not take a look in the kitchen? Billy wanted me to look around, right? Slowly, I opened the door and stuck my head in. All I saw was the big island in the middle of the kitchen before the young man came out of a pantry on the other side of the room with a roll in his mouth and one in each hand.

When he saw me, he somehow managed to get the one in his mouth into one of his hands, and he said, "You looking for the bathroom? It's through the other door." He was out of his sweatsuit and was wearing jeans and an oily shirt.

"Yes, thank you very much!" I hoped that I looked innocent, because I wasn't. I so wasn't.

Stepping back out the door, I opened the other one. It opened out to a long hallway. The first door I came to on the left was a weight room. Nothing to see there. The next room on the right was a library of grand proportions showing off floor-to-ceiling bookcases on all four walls. A big rolltop desk sat over to the left, with not a thing on it. The next door to the right was the bathroom. It was as big as Aiden's bedroom and had a double sink and a porcelain fake-old-time bathtub that was beautiful.

When I finished in the bathroom and was coming out the door that led to the dining room, it surprised me to see Billy and Amanda in the entranceway shaking hands. He had tricked me! Billy had already conducted the interview while I was in the bathroom. He tricked me!

CHAPTER TWENTY

I SMILED A goodbye to Amanda and glared at Billy who gave an almost imperceptible shrug of his shoulders. We got outside the front door, and I gave Billy's big shoulder a shove. "You tricked me! You never were going to let me in on the interview, were you?"

He turned toward me and put his hand on my shoulder, but I pulled away from him. "Lorry, you are not a detective and you are not a deputy. You are my *girlfriend*. And girlfriends don't attend interviews with murder suspects. I shouldn't have even let you in her house, so you should be glad you could go at all." He walked toward the car like the matter was settled.

As soon as I got in the car, he put the key in the ignition, but I pushed his hand away. "Wait! Tell me—is she still a suspect?"

"No, she isn't. She had a gas receipt dated Monday morning at 7:30 at a Scottsdale station. She couldn't have been two places at once. Rutledge is hours away." He raised his eyebrows, nodded once, and started the car.

That seemed too simple. Something didn't feel right. I

liked her and all, but just because you like someone, doesn't mean you can let them get away with murder. It isn't the right thing to do. It was then that I noticed an old classic Jaguar parked on the other side of the driveway, with the young man's head leaned in under the hood. "Billy, drive up to him. I want to ask him something." When Billy hesitated, I said, "Something about the car." Notice I did not say whose car.

Billy pulled up beside him, and Billy said, "Just roll down the window and ask him from here." I don't think he trusted me. Smart man. He pushed a button, and my window rolled down. I opened my door before he had a chance to hit the lock button. But it was unfortunate that the window was down, as he could hear everything I said.

"Uh, hi!" I stepped up next to the car. It was a deep blue with white pin striping. "Can I ask you something?"

He picked his head up and narrowly missed whacking it on the hood. "Yeah, sure. Is this about the ticket that Amanda got with my car? Because I had nothing to do with that."

Luckily, he had forgotten that Billy and his car were from Rutledge County and not Mariposa County. "Ah, what ticket?"

"The one she got Monday. We swapped cars for a day. Hers was bone dry when I started it! I barely made it to the gas station!"

"What time did you get gas?"

"Seven-thirty Monday morning over at that Shell Station on East Dynamite."

Having acquired the information I wanted, I switched to more pleasant topics. "So is this a '61? Sure is a beaut!"

"Hey! You know your cars! Do you like it?" He beamed. Guys always like it when you compliment their cars.

"I've never seen one nicer."

"Yeah, me either. That's why I bought it—well, actually my dad bought it for my birthday," he confessed.

"What a grrrreat birthday present!"

"Yeah, I thought so!"

"Well, thanks."

He smiled warmly at me and stuck his head back under the hood. Billy glared at me when I got in the car, but didn't say a word until he had rolled up my window.

"You lied to me!"

I looked at him and gave him my innocent face. At least I thought it was my innocent face, but it might have been my revenge face that sneaked in. "No, I didn't. We talked about the car." Then I glared back at him. "Besides, *you* lied to me!"

Billy straightened up and stared straight ahead. "I did not. *Never* did I say you could be there while I interviewed the suspect. I said you could go with me to the valley."

Then I looked out the window and noticed that Billy was going south on the 101 instead of north or west on side streets. "Where are we going?"

He smiled at me then, the tension between us gone. "I have a special treat for you!"

I smiled and then glanced at my watch. "Oh, no! Aiden!"

"Isn't Petra taking care of him?"

"Until five, but she wasn't sure after that." I dug into my purse to find my cell phone and tapped the number for the historical society. "Petra? . . . Hi. . . . Can you

94

babysit Aiden tonight? . . . Oh, it's been that busy? Bummer. . . . Is he there now? . . . Okay, I'll let you know who will pick him up. . . . Thanks."

After pressing the *End Call* button, I said, "Petra can't do it because it's been busy, and she needs to study. I'll try Martha." I tapped the numbers and waited for an answer. "Martha Goldstein, please. . . .Thank you. . . . Martha? Hi, it's Lorry. Remember I told you I'd be out of the office today? I'm going to be back late, and I was wondering if you and Hugo could watch Aiden for a couple of hours. . . . Oh, you are? . . . All right, that's okay. Thanks!" Turning to Billy, I said, "They're going out tonight. I'll try Zack."

Since I knew Zack didn't like getting phone calls at work, I tapped a message into the phone and sent the text. A few minutes later, I got a response, *Sorry, Lorry, I have a class tonight.* After tapping in a thank you, I said, "No luck." I looked at Billy and frowned. Then we both said together, "Bryan."

Quickly, I tapped more numbers into the phone and said, "Keep your fingers crossed." Billy held up his hand with his index and second finger crossed which made me smile. Then Bryan answered the phone. "Hi, Bryan! It's Lorry. I was wondering if there was any chance you and Ryan could babysit Aiden tonight? . . . You can? Awesome! I'm so grateful! . . . Oh, cool. . . . Oh, Billy and I are down in the valley. . . . Yeah, but he wouldn't let me help him interview the suspect! . . . Yeah, oh well. . . . What time should I tell Petra you'll be there? . . . Oh, that's great. . . . Thank you! . . . Bye."

Turning toward Billy and letting out a huge sigh, I said, "They can do it. He also said he has a surprise for Aiden that he's been meaning to bring down."

"Did he say what it was?" Billy asked, a tiny edge to his voice that probably only I would recognize.

Bryan O'Keefe had been my attorney for the brief time I was suspected of murder. Since I was never charged, he didn't have that big of a role, but my mother's attorneys in Minnesota hired him to help me. And while he was helping me get a new car and all the other happenings associated with the murder, we became friends.

But at some point, Billy and I, who were a couple by then, discovered that Bryan was gay. The first time I suggested that Bryan and his boyfriend, Ryan, who moved to Flagstaff from Minnesota to be with him, babysit Aiden, Billy put up a huge fuss. I had to keep reminding Billy that just because someone is gay doesn't make him a child molester. Talk about judgmental! Finally Billy acquiesced, but only if he could have *the talk* with Aiden to warn him of monsters that might be lurking out among the public. The first night that Bryan and Ryan babysat, Billy and I had gone to the movies in Coyote Moon, and Billy was so nervous that I don't think he ever watched the movie.

When we got home and everything was fine, and Aiden was happy and untouched, Billy still wasn't satisfied. So he insisted on signing Aiden up for karate lessons, and he signed himself up, too—in the adult class —so Aiden wouldn't suspect anything. Every Wednesday, Billy would go with Aiden to his lesson, and every Thursday, Aiden would go with Billy to his. They were both yellow belts now, but it thrilled Aiden to no end that he got his first. Anyway, Billy accepted Bryan and Ryan after that and was much more comfortable with them— as a couple—but still a little wary. We've barbecued with them and had them over, but Billy still isn't comfortable when they sit for Aiden.

"I don't know what the surprise is, Billy, but I'm sure it's fine."

He sighed, nodded, and tightened his lips. "Oh, here we are."

CHAPTER TWENTY-ONE

"A PARK IS my treat?" While I had been busy on the phone, Billy had gotten off the 101 and driven to the park.

"Yeah, wait till you see it."

He pulled into the parking lot. "Look, *grass*! We can walk barefoot on the grass! And look behind us! A lake! How cool is that?" Billy turned off the engine, opened his door, and took off his boots.

"Wait a minute. I have to call Petra." Quickly I tapped in the number, told her about Bryan, and ended the call. Then I opened my door and slipped off my heels. It wouldn't be my bare feet because I had on nylons, but it would be close. There was no way I was going to slip off my pantyhose!

I stepped out of the car and walked gingerly across the parking lot to the grass in front of it. The wind was blowing my dress around, so I had to hold my arms on it to keep it from revealing my underwear. When I put my feet on the grass, I sighed. Even through the nylons, it felt good. "Oh, Billy, this is great."

He put his arms around me, kissed me, released me,

and pointed behind us. "See there? Do you want to walk by the lake?"

I saw the water, but it was the palm trees by the lake that caught my attention. There weren't that many of them, a few to our right and one to the left, but every one of them had their top leaves stretched out in the wind. It was still blowing my dress, and besides, I saw several geese walking along the edge of the lake and didn't want to step in any goose poop, so I said, "No, let's walk on the grass over here. It feels so good! You're right, Billy. This is a great treat!"

Billy wanted to hold my hand as we walked, and as much as I wanted to, I couldn't. If I stopped holding my skirt down, it flew up around my face and revealed all that I didn't want revealed. Don't ask how I know that. I looked up and saw the clouds hanging heavy above us. "Looks like it might rain," I said.

He smiled and kissed me on the forehead. "Don't worry. We won't melt."

As we walked, we talked about the interview he had stolen from me. "So what did she say, anyway? You know, besides the phony gas receipt."

"She said she hadn't seen Charles Jones in more than a year, and she had called him to wish him a happy birthday. When I said that I knew she had called him more than just the one day, she tearfully confessed that she missed him and just wanted to talk."

"Do you believe her?"

Billy shook his head. "I don't know what to think, honestly. She seemed nice enough. But as you know, some killers are."

"Yes, that's for sure. Well, I liked her, too. She was friendly and warm. But, like you say, that doesn't

99

preclude her from being a killer."

He nodded. "Yeah, well, I'll know more when I check on that ticket. If she got it in Prescott or Cottonwood at the right time—well, you know. But if she got it here in the valley somewhere, then that's her alibi, and it would be solid."

"Yeah, a ticket here in the valley would be airtight, wouldn't it? Although that makes one wonder why would she lie?"

Billy smiled at me a conspiratorial little smile. "I think she has another boyfriend and didn't want to admit it." He looked at me and winked. "And honestly, if I had left you alone to ask her a few questions, she probably would have told *you* the truth."

"See? I could have helped you!" I gave him a playful shove. "You blew it, big boy!"

He turned me toward him and put his arms around me again. "*You*," he hesitated to emphasize it, "are my girlfriend, not my deputy. You're not a detective. You need to leave the heavy lifting to us detectives!"

I didn't want to mention it was with my help that he solved his last two cases. He knew it, I knew it, and there was no need to remind him of it. So I looked up at him, smiled, and let him kiss me again. Because I liked it.

We started walking again, but I turned us to head back to the car. The wind was still blowing, and it was getting annoying that I had to keep holding my dress down. I could have just not held it down and let everyone see my pretty pink undies, but I didn't think that would be appropriate for the girlfriend of a county sheriff. Imagine the town people talking! But we weren't in town and, well, who would know?

As I was considering the possibility, a big gust of wind

threw me off balance. And it had to be a *big* gust of wind because I'm no lightweight. I grabbed for Billy and as I said, I'm no lightweight, and between me and the big gust, it threw him off balance, too. We were both laughing until I looked over his shoulder to see what was coming at us and coming fast.

A haboob. A giant haboob coming straight for us. I found out its name later, but not knowing its name at the time didn't make it any less scary.

CHAPTER TWENTY-TWO

"BILLY, LOOK!" I stood there frozen in place. There was a giant wall of red dust closing in like a tidal wave and getting closer every second.

Billy took one look and screamed, "Lorry! Run for the car! Hurry!" As I took off running, my skirt flew up to my shoulders, but I didn't care who saw what. I just kept running. When Billy saw that I was heading toward the passenger side, he yelled, "No! *My* side! Quickly!"

Billy got there first and opened the door for me. I jumped in, he tossed me his keys, pressed a button on the door and then closed it. The dust had already reached the passenger side of the car and covered the windows. Billy barely made it into the back seat before the dust engulfed the whole car. There was a small bush a few feet in front of the car, and I couldn't see it. I couldn't see *anything*—anything except dust, that is. It was so disorienting that it almost felt like we were underwater. So I couldn't help it and took great gulps of air making me hyperventilate. That made me want to barf, but it also made me want to go outside, and since I felt lightheaded from the hyperventilation, I didn't know any better and reached for the door handle to step outside into the maelstrom.

"Lorry! Don't open that door!"

Taking my hand away, I said, "Oh!" and looked in the rearview mirror.

"Are you okay?" He reached his hand out for me, but the glass between us stopped him.

"No. Not really. I'm scared, Billy."

"It's okay, honey. I'll take care of you. We're safe now, as long as you don't open the door."

"Can't we leave and get out of here?" Okay, it was a stupid question, but giant dust storms always made me stupid. And not to mention being lightheaded.

"You know we can't. We can't even see that bush in front of the car." Billy noticed that, too. Not much gets past that man.

"What is it? What's going on? I've never seen anything like it."

"It's called a haboob. It's a giant dust storm. Phoenix gets 'em sometimes. A friend who lives down here says they used to call them dust storms, but when they got bigger, they started calling them haboobs."

I took a deep breath and tried to calm myself. It wasn't cold, but I was shivering, so I crossed my arms over my chest and rubbed both my upper arms. "What's a haboob?"

"Let me see if I can get reception with this thing going on." He held up his cell phone and moved it around to different positions all around him.

"Who ya gonna call?"

"Haboob busters!" said Billy and then laughed. I hadn't seen the movie he referred to, so I didn't get it. "I'm just looking up haboob on the 'net. It says haboob is an Arabic word that means strong wind. They normally happen around monsoon season, but it's not that unusual for them to come at other times of the year. You know how we haven't had any rain for a few months? That just makes this worse."

"It looked like a huge tidal wave of red dust. How high do you think it was?"

"A couple thousand feet, at least, I'd say."

While we were talking, I could hear sand and debris hitting the car. Every time a big piece hit and made a *plunk* sound, I jumped. Strong gusts of wind sometimes made the car sway. I felt like a rabbit trapped in a cage while someone or some thing shook the cage and threw stuff at me.

"What if I have to go to the bathroom?" I asked.

"You don't. You just went."

"What happens if I do? How long do these things last? Another five minutes or something?"

Billy was still tapping away on his phone. "Doubtful. I read on one site it could last an hour and on another site, it said it could last three hours. But the three hours was rare."

Both hands flung up to my face, and I scrunched my eyes together so I wouldn't cry. "Oh, Billy, I can't do three hours of this. Really. I can't."

"Honey, there's nothing I can do. There's nothing in my power I can do to make it stop. I'm sorry. But at least we're together."

"No, we're not," I whined. "You're in the back, and I'm in the front. Can I come back there with you?"

"Lorry, dear," Billy said with clenched teeth, "you can't open the door with this going on. If you have to go to the bathroom, cross your legs."

I was about to burst into tears, but I didn't see the profit in it. Whining was bad enough. I felt like such a victim, a powerless put-upon victim. And Billy wouldn't even feel sorry for me, because he was going through the same thing that I was. And he wasn't even scared. Sometimes I hated that about him, and other times— most of the time—I wouldn't have it any other way. Right now, I hated it. He was taking everything so nonchalantly like he went through a haboob every day and there was nothing to worry about, and I hated that.

I sat there fuming a few more minutes and then looked over my right shoulder to the rifle pointed straight up. Well, if they declared martial law, I knew we'd be safe.

Looking around, there was no visibility from any window in the car. The windows on the passenger side of the car were still being pelted by sand and who knows what else. The other windows just got hit when the wind gusted. I sat there on edge, while Billy continued looking at his cell phone and periodically reciting facts about haboobs, like haboobs have been compared to dust storms on Mars. Look out the window, man! Live it! But he just clicked onward. It made me wonder if maybe he was a little scared after all. He usually wasn't into surfing on his cell phone like this. Then again, what else was there to do?

And then, suddenly, it was over, and heavy sheets of rain poured down from the sky. Thunder wracked the car, and lightning lit up the skies, but the dust was gone. The rain turned the dust to mud and covered the windshield and windows of the car, but it was coming down so hard that it was washing it away just as fast.

CHAPTER TWENTY-THREE

CLOSING MY EYES, I took a deep breath and thought how grateful I was that the haboob was over. Billy was still hunched over his cell phone. He had to sit crooked, because his long legs wouldn't fit behind the seat.

"Billy?"

"Yeah, yeah, I know the haboob blew by." He tapped one more thing into the phone. "Can you get into the passenger seat?"

"Not from here!" There was a tiny space between the computer in the front seat and the back partition. Well, it was tiny compared to the big butt that would have to get by it. *My* big butt that is.

"I didn't mean crawl over. You'd have to be about as big as Aiden for that! I meant open the door and go around."

"It's raining!"

"I can see that it's raining, Lorry, but you can't drive us home, and I'm not going to sit back here for all those hours."

"Well, don't you have an umbrella or something?" I was exasperated. First the haboob and now the rain.

"There's one in the back, but by the time I got it out, I would be soaking wet."

While I watched him in the rearview mirror, he turned with his hand out as if to open the door. "Shoot!" he said. "I forgot where I was. You're going to have to retrieve those keys I threw to you and unlock the door for me."

The keys had ricocheted off my breast and landed on the floor. Since Billy had been sitting in the driver's seat, I had plenty of room to bend over and pick them up. Turning around, I held them up and shook them until Billy looked up. "Or, I can drive us home, and you'll just have to be a passenger. Can you get your seat belt on?" I smiled at him and blinked my eyes coquettishly.

"Lor-ry," he said, drawing it out between his teeth with a sour expression on his face.

"Okay! Okay! How do I hand them to you?"

"You can't. You have to unlock the door for me."

Reluctantly, I opened the front door. Billy's boots were lying there, soaked. I had accidentally kicked them over when I jumped into the car. "Oops. Sorry about your boots, Billy." Stepping out of the car, I unlocked the door for him and then ran for the passenger side. The inside of one of my thighs didn't get too wet. The rest of me got soaked.

Billy had gotten in the driver's side, and he held up his dripping boots. "Can you put them on your side? There's no room over here."

"There's no room over here, either! Oh, all right!" And I took the boots and put them as close to the door and as far away from me as I could get them.

Billy sat there, hair dripping into his eyes and watching me. When I picked my head up after arranging the

107

boots, I looked at him looking at me. The water was dripping off my hair into my eyes, too.

He smiled at me. "What a pair we make, huh?" Reaching behind the computer terminal, he squeezed my shoulder. "This was a grand adventure for us, wasn't it?"

"I'm not sure I'd call it that, Billy."

"You know, to tell the grandkids and stuff." He took his hand off my shoulder and started the car.

Those words hit me so hard that I couldn't respond. We had only been *dating* for a few months, and I'd only known him a few months before that. Marriage and children had never come up before. But although we'd only been together for a brief time, I knew if he ever asked, I would say yes. You know why? I had a comparison, baby! Eddie was the worst husband ever. And Billy was nothing like him. Billy in every way and in everything he did and said was a good man, and I trusted him completely. I could never have said that about Eddie. I never trusted him. Then why would I marry a man like that? Right now, I have no idea. You'll have to ask my self of ten years ago to get that answer.

Billy pulled onto the 101 heading toward I-17. Soon, I saw one of those big signs with changeable messages. Today's message said *20 min to I-17.*

Looking at my watch, I groaned. It would be hours before we got home. Then I brightened. "Billy? How about checking out Amanda Fletcher's ticket?"

He checked his rearview mirror, the side mirror, and turned his head toward the back. Then he moved the car over several lanes and pulled onto the side of the freeway.

"What are you doing?"

108

"Checking her ticket. That's a good idea."

"Why'd you have to pull over?"

Both of his hands were on the keyboard, and he looked over the monitor at me. "Distracted driving, my dear. I don't do it." His hands moved fast on the keyboard—he must have taken typing in school. "Ah, here it is. Speeding ticket, Scottsdale, 6:30 A.M. Monday. I guess that clears her."

"Why do you think she lied?"

"About getting gas? Like I said before, my guess is that she has a new boyfriend in Scottsdale somewhere. It doesn't matter. She didn't kill Charles Jones."

"Curious," I shook my head, not really understanding people.

"Lor, not everyone who lies is a killer. Lots of times people lie for their own reasons. I never take a lie as proof of guilt."

Billy pulled smoothly out into traffic, and a few minutes later, we merged onto I-17 north. Between the swish, swish, swish of the windshield wipers and the rain beating down, I fell asleep before we had even passed the Outlet Mall. And I didn't wake up again until I felt the car slowing hours later.

"What? Huh?" I blinked my eyes as we were taking the exit for AZ-260.

"You hungry? I'm starved."

"Yeah, I am hungry now that you mention it. All that sleeping is hard work."

The rain had stopped, and Billy pulled into a Carl's Jr drive-thru and stopped at the microphone for ordering to go. He ordered for both of us, he paid, he drove to the parking lot, and we ate our hamburgers and French fries.

When he finished, he patted his stomach. "That's

better now. Shall we proceed home, my lady?"

"Yes, we shall, kind sir." I smiled at him. "Thank you for dinner, for lunch, and for an adventurous day!" I hoped he wouldn't bring up the grandkids again, because that would have made me uncomfortable. But he didn't, and I was glad.

Neither of us spoke again until we were driving through Coyote Moon on the last part of our journey. Although that was probably because I fell asleep five minutes after we left Carl's Jr.

"So what do you think the surprise is?" asked Billy, when he saw me moving again.

"I don't know, but I'm sure it's nothing to be worried about."

"I'm not worried," he said, but his voice betrayed him when it went up an octave or two. "Well, not since he started taking karate."

"He's just a yellow belt, Billy. I don't think he could take out a kindergartner on crutches! Not that he would, of course."

"Lorry, you need to come see him in class. He may be a yellow belt, but it's name only. He'd be much farther along if they'd let him test for it, but they won't. He's farther along than I am!"

"Seriously? But I thought you were also a yellow belt?"

"I am. That's the point. If they'd let him test, he would no longer be a yellow belt. The kid is good!"

It made me think I should probably go with them to karate class sooner rather than later. I hadn't gone up to now, because I thought it was a good time for Billy and Aiden to do some male bonding, and they didn't need me along for that. But Billy asking me about the surprise, and the note of worry in his voice, made me remember one of the first times we had left Aiden with Bryan and Ryan. We ended up coming home early from the movie, and when we walked in the house, Bryan was on the couch with Aiden, reading him a story. Ryan was on the floor on his back, and Bingo was on his chest panting with his tongue lolling out. When Bingo saw us come through the door, instead of running to greet us like he usually did, he flopped down on Ryan's chest and just wagged his tail. The scene was so funny that Billy and I cracked up. But tonight, it was a different scene we walked into.

CHAPTER TWENTY-FOUR

WE UNLOCKED THE front door and walked in. Often, the three of them would be on the couch eating popcorn and watching one of Aiden's movies with Bingo in someone's lap. But tonight, the TV was off and the living room was dark. Billy and I looked at each other, then took a few more steps. The light was on in the kitchen, and we saw Bryan, Ryan, and Aiden huddled around the kitchen table with Bingo at Aiden's feet, his tongue lolling.

"What's going on here?" Billy asked.

Aiden didn't even look up. "Ryan got me a new game. I've already won twice." He was on his knees on the chair so he could reach the far corner of the game board. It was a big picture of the United States, with many of the cities labeled and marked with red and different color rectangles going between the cities. Little plastic train cars sat on some of the rectangles.

We learned, between moves, that Ryan had gotten Aiden a new game called Ticket to Ride. Bryan explained that at first Ryan had bought Aiden the children's version, but Bryan insisted that he return it and get the adult version. And considering that Aiden had already won two games, it was a good choice.

Billy and I stood there watching, Billy's arm casually over my shoulders, until they finished the game. This time, Ryan won. Aiden wanted to play again, but it felt late, and I didn't want to keep Bryan and Ryan any longer. They still had to drive back to Flagstaff—Flag to the locals. I tried to pay them like I always tried to pay them, and they always turned down the money. One of them would always say, "What? Get paid to spend time with a friend? No way! We should pay you!" And then whoever said it would tousle Aiden's hair, Aiden would hug him, and they would leave, everyone with smiles on their faces.

After they left, Aiden taught me and Billy to play Ticket to Ride, and it was fun—much more fun than Uncle Wiggly. But it was tough, too. Aiden beat us both, although Billy was a close second. Then we put Aiden to bed, read to him, and turned out his light.

Both of us flopped onto the couch, with Billy's arm around me, and we talked about the day. From the interview to the haboob to how much fun we always have together. Nothing was said about him not letting me in on the interview or me talking to the guy with the car. Nothing needed to be said. We worked it out like we always do. That's how it was with me and Billy—we always worked it out.

Billy stood up. "I need to leave early, babe. It's not only been a long day, but I have to go in early to meet with John Brannigan. He wanted to come in before school."

"Why couldn't he call you?"

Billy shook his head. "Don't know." Then he headed

toward the door.

Billy left after kissing me goodnight, and I collapsed into bed and immediately fell asleep.

The following morning, I was awakened by Aiden and Bingo jumping on my bed. "C'mon, Mommy! Get up!" Aiden chirped. Bingo barked. I rolled over.

"Mom, it's late. I'm going to be late for school. You need to get up, or I'll have to make my own lunch! Seventeen Double Stuffs! C'mon!"

Through eyes still squinty from sleep, I looked at the clock. Aiden was right. It was late. We had to leave in fifteen minutes. Jumping out of bed, as I ran through the door toward the kitchen, I said, "Hurry! Get dressed. I'll go make your lunch!"

I raced into the kitchen, put a bowl, a spoon, cereal, and milk on the table, and then I started on his lunch. This week was cheese and salami in a pita. I put the tomato and lettuce in a separate plastic bag, and half a peeled cucumber in another, added two—and only two —Double Stuff cookies, and rolled the bag closed. Bingo was at my feet looking up at me with pleading eyes, so I poured food in his dish and put water in to make it more palatable. Bingo looked grateful and began eating. Aiden came in with his shirt untucked. "Tuck your shirt in before you put your sweatshirt on." Then I poured his milk into his cereal and raced back into the bedroom to get myself dressed.

After opening my closet, I pulled out the two things on the end. An A-line black skirt, and a white, frilly blouse. It would make me look like Brandi at the library who always dresses in black and white because she thinks she used to be a pilgrim. And guess whose idea it was to give her books on reincarnation? Aiden's, that's who.

114

Sometimes I think that kid just reads too much. Wait. No, I don't think that at all. But maybe I could pay more attention to what he's reading. Censor his books? No, I don't think so. It seems like it would be the right thing to do to only let him read books that reflect *my* beliefs, but that's not allowing him to become the person he's becoming. For that reason alone, I would never censor his books. I won't allow him to read *Fifty Shades of Gray* when he's seven, or other books of that ilk, but other than that he has free rein to read anything he wants. And that is as it should be.

As I got dressed, Bingo came into the room, and I let him out the back sliding door. He was already scratching at the back door before I finished buttoning my blouse. After I opened the door for him, he ran into the living room when Aiden called him. Sliding my feet into my black heels, I grabbed my purse and ran out to the living room. Aiden already had his sweatshirt and jacket on, and he was carrying his backpack. Bingo was jumping up and down trying to get his leash from where it hung on the wall.

"C'mon, hurry," I said. "We're late." I backed out of the house and turned the deadbolt from the outside. Billy had installed it a few months before and insisted that I use it. Then I turned around to go to my car, and there was no car! I had forgotten that I had left it at the historical society. Luckily, Billy didn't forget, and there he was standing outside his patrol car with his arms crossed across his chest, and a big smile on his face.

CHAPTER TWENTY-FIVE

"SHERIFF BILLY!" AIDEN shouted and ran into his arms. Billy swung him around.

"Guess what, kiddo? *You* get to ride in the back of my patrol car just like a regular criminal! How cool is that?"

"Really cool!" Aiden said as he climbed into the back and patted his lap for Bingo to follow.

After making sure Aiden had his seat belt on, Billy closed the back door, smiled at me, and then kissed me. "Am I good or what?"

I nodded to him. "Oh, you're definitely good!"

We both got in the car, and Billy turned around to check on Aiden. Then he started the car and pulled out into the street.

"Sheriff Billy?" Aiden asked from the back seat. "Why is there glass and heavy metal screening between me and you?"

"Because we have to keep the criminal element from being able to reach the officer in the front seat."

"Why are these seats so uncomfortable?"

Aiden was referring to the hard plastic molded back seat. I had sat in one before. He was right. It was very uncomfortable. It also brought back terrible memories.

"Because it makes them easy to clean. And if you want to know why they would need to be easy to clean, you'll have to use your imagination. I don't want to gross out your mother!"

Billy smiled at me, and Aiden laughed. "Okay, Sheriff Billy. I get it." Then he laughed again.

A minute later, Billy pulled up in front of the school. "You getting out of the back of a patrol car will give you some attention. Think you can handle it?"

"Sure can!" Aiden felt along the side panel of the car. "How do I get out?"

"You don't until I get you out, little pard! Remember, the back seat is a place where I transport criminals, and you're playing the part, right?"

Aiden raised both hands in the air. "Don't shoot, Sheriff Billy! I didn't do it! I promise!"

Billy laughed, got out of the car, and walked to the other side. When he opened the door, Aiden still had his hands up. Bingo barked again and squealed when Billy retrieved him from Aiden's lap. Aiden exited the car with his hands up.

"You better grab your backpack there, little pard. Or I will have to take you in for negligence at the start of your day."

Aiden laughed, took Bingo out of Billy's arms, put him in the back seat, and grabbed his backpack. I opened the passenger door and put my arms out to Aiden. He came up to me, hugged me, kissed me on the cheek, smiled, and ran into school, still laughing.

"I swear, you make that kid's day!"

"*Every* day!" Billy said as he opened the back door, took Bingo out again, and handed him to me. "Bingo isn't a criminal, and I don't think he wants to pretend he's one, so you take him."

I hugged Bingo, and Billy closed my door, walked around, and stepped into the car. A minute later, he pulled into the back of the historical society. When I reached for the door, he stopped me.

"I have to show you something." He pulled a piece of paper out of his top pocket and handed it to me.

It was a photocopy of a small note. It said, *Maybe I should just "take care" of her, huh? LOL Then we could be together all the time!*

"What's this? I don't get it. Who's it from and who is it to?"

Billy looked at me with a frown on his face. "John found it in Kasey's drawer. He thought it was a note for her boyfriend that she never got to give him."

"I still don't get it. It says *LOL*—laugh out loud— doesn't that mean she was just joking?"

"Lorry, it's a murder investigation. *LOL* doesn't count in this case. She joked about *taking care of her*—which I assume to be Chuck Jones's wife—and *taking care of* doesn't mean bringing her tea and cookies! This isn't good, Lorry. Seriously. What it means to me and any decent lawyer who got hold of it is that Kasey had murder on her mind, and if she had it on her mind once, what's to stop her from having it on her mind again?"

"Why did John even bring that to you? Um, can't you get rid of it?"

"Lorry, I'm going to pretend you didn't say that, because you know that is something I would never do."

Embarrassed, I looked down at the note in my hands. Billy was right. I knew he would never do anything like that. But I didn't think Kasey murdered anybody, so why

118

put something out there that would make her look even more guilty than she already looked? I thought about that again. If Kasey was actually thinking of killing Chuck's wife, maybe she *was* capable of killing him—if he was going to break up with her or something. Just because she was my cousin didn't mean that she wasn't capable of murder. Like Billy said early on, cousins can kill, too. Maybe Kasey wasn't innocent after all.

CHAPTER TWENTY-SIX

SINCE I DIDN'T have breakfast and had spent a restless night dreaming of getting caught in haboobs, I checked in with Petra and then walked next door to the cafe to get some food and mass quantities of coffee. When I walked in, it surprised me that almost every table was full. I walked up to the counter, and Kasey came up to me. I hadn't seen her since I dropped her off at her house two days before.

She didn't smile. "Hello, Lorry. Checking on your investment? Did you come to see if I was still here?" Kasey frowned and looked around. "Well, for your information, they were going to fire me until they realized my presence here was good for business." She used her chin to motion around the room, and then she sighed. "So what can I get for you?"

"An egg mcmuffin and an extra large coffee."

Kasey closed her eyes and sighed more deeply. "Lorry, this isn't the golden arches. What do you want?"

"Don't you have something *like* an egg mcmuffin? Like an egg on a croissant or something?"

"Yeah, yeah, all right." She scribbled something on a

120

pad, ripped off the top sheet, and put it on the rack behind her. Then, without looking at me, she walked around the counter to pour more coffee for people at the tables.

I never thought I'd say this, but I missed the old talkative, smiling, good natured Kasey. She may have talked a lot, but she seemed a lot happier, and she was easier to deal with. Who wants to deal with the sourpuss she had become? I took a deep breath and looked around.

Wait a minute. How happy was I when I was accused of murder? Not very happy, I'm sure. Can I really blame Kasey for not smiling like she used to? Not only was her boyfriend murdered, and she accused of it, but now she had to deal with the realities of her husband knowing about it. Yes, he knew about it before, but it was still a "secret" so they didn't have to talk about it. Now it was out in the open. That couldn't be a good thing. Poor Kasey. Color me ashamed. I needed to have more compassion and less judgment. But believe me, that is more difficult than it sounds.

Kasey brought the coffee and croissant and slapped them and the bill in front of me. She walked off before I had a chance to pay it. Before I left, I put more money than was necessary on top of the bill and walked out. I knew a large tip wouldn't change things between us, but it was a start. When I got to the door, I turned around to look at her, but she had disappeared into the back.

After I scarfed down the croissant and sipped contentedly at my coffee, I checked my email. Nothing from Martha and no envelopes of typing on my desk. I wiped my face on the napkin and walked to Petra's desk.

"Hey, Petra."

"Hey," she said without looking up. She wore a sweater that was two sizes too large, and a skirt that was one size too small. But who was I to judge? I wore three-inch heels that I would continue to wear even when it snowed.

"Aiden and I decided which exhibit to phase out. I'm going upstairs now to pick one to bring down."

"Yeah, all right."

I stepped into the bathroom to *powder my nose*, and then I hiked upstairs to where the exhibits were. Since I didn't remember seeing any exhibits in the places I had visited upstairs, I started at the back and circled the room. When I walked by the shelves on the wall by the staircase, Rocky stood up, stretched, and looked at me. He wanted to jump in my arms, but as much as I loved the cat, that just wasn't my thing. Meanwhile, I saw nothing that could be exhibits. Then I looked down all the aisles, and I still saw nothing. Where could they be? I checked everywhere I had just been and still I found nothing, so I traipsed back downstairs.

"Petra? Where are the old exhibits? I didn't see them anywhere."

"Did you go to the room above the cafe? I think they're in there."

"Above the cafe? What do you mean?"

"When the cafe took over that third of the building, they only wanted the downstairs, so the upstairs above the cafe is still ours. There's a door at the front of the room on the side where the cafe is. It's probably locked, but your key will unlock it. Lemme know if you don't find it." She had never turned toward me and typed the entire time she talked. Petra was dedicated and consistent, that was for sure.

I retrieved the key from my purse and trudged back upstairs. If I got any more exercise than this, I might lose weight and fade right away. Oh, wait. Probably not.

Using the key, I let myself in. There was a big window so there was plenty of light. And someone had placed a chair in front of the old exhibits. How convenient. This wouldn't take any time at all. I sat down to go through them.

There was a small one that was a timeline of Rutledge including when Wyatt Earp stayed here. Since I didn't believe it, I passed that one by. One that I was sure that Aiden would like was of the Rutledge Fire Department. Not only did they have some cool pictures of the old Fire Department, but they had an old fire engine model replete with a Dalmatian sitting in the front seat. Another cool one was the original blueprint for the historical society along with an aerial shot of early Rutledge, more than a century ago. Moving the chair, I saw that the next one was an old switchboard with the cables and all, plus an old Rutledge telephone book that was paper thin. That was cool, too.

I was about to move on to the next box when I heard something. Was it the cat? Bingo was at my feet, and he heard it, too. He looked toward the door and barked. It wasn't the cat. Bingo wouldn't have barked at Rocky; he loved that cat. I stood up and walked out the door into the main upstairs room of the historical society. Then I heard her. Petra calling me.

"Lorry! Can't you hear me? Did you close the friggin' door? Lorry! C'mon! I don't want to walk up there! I have work to do!"

Walking to the top of the stairs, I stood there with my hands on my hips. Sometimes Petra's dedication to her

123

studies annoyed me. It shouldn't. She wasn't here to work, she was just here to use the computer and have some place besides home to study. Plus, she often covered for me when she didn't have to. But she was here, and I sometimes forgot that she wasn't working. My own fault, really.

"Yes, Petra. What!"

Petra sighed, loud enough for me to hear upstairs, and then shook her head. "It's your *boyfriend*. He wants to talk to you, and he says it's important."

Although it was true that I usually answered my own phone, still, it was very unusual for Billy to leave a message like that. Concerned, I raced down the stairs, with Bingo barking at my heels.

CHAPTER TWENTY-SEVEN

WHEN I GOT to my desk, the phone was on the hook. "Petra? Where's Billy?"

"At the sheriff's station, I assume."

"I mean the phone! I thought he was on the phone!"

"He told me to give you the message, and then he hung up."

"Well, you could have said so!"

"I just did," she said in a haughty sort of way.

After I tapped in the number for the sheriff's station, I still had to wait several minutes, so I put the speaker phone on so I wouldn't have to hold the phone up to my ear for so long. Billy came on the phone and without preamble, he demanded, "Where were you?"

"Um, *excuse* me," I said. "I raced down the stairs in my three-inch heels, called you immediately, and then had to wait. So I ask you, 'Where were *you*?'" Maybe I should shut up about my three-inch heels. Billy was probably getting tired of hearing about them, and everybody else probably was, too.

"Oh, jeez, Lorry, I'm sorry. It's just—well, there's so much going on here. I'm sorry."

"It's okay, Billy. What was so important?"

"Oh! Yeah! That's why I called! Listen, Lorry, it's not good."

"More evidence that Kasey killed him? That doesn't surprise me."

"No, not Kasey. John."

"*John?* No way. I don't see that at all. Kasey, maybe. John definitely no. What makes you even *think* that?"

"Just now, Derek was outside and came in just after an anonymous telephone message came in. He came into my office, waving the message and demanding that I go down to the school and pick up John. And if I didn't want to, then he intended to do it himself—with his siren on and guns a-blazing—and drag John out in handcuffs."

"He said that? Really?"

"Almost exactly that."

"What was he doing outside, anyway?"

"Lorry, I don't know what he was doing outside. He's not the suspect! John is!"

"Well, does he smoke or what?"

"John? No, he doesn't smoke. You know that."

"No, not John! Derek. He's the one who was outside. Does he smoke?"

"Lorry, this is ridiculous. Give the kid a break. He's still upset that his sister's husband was killed. That's all. So, anyway, where I was going with this is that I called John, and he's coming back in so I can question him again. And I might have to book him."

"What did the message say?"

"The caller said they had seen John coming out of the post office and running down the street."

"That's all?"

126

"That's enough! Anyway, Lorry, I've got to go. I just wanted to let you know that. I have my hands full here. As soon as I got Derek calmed down, he went into the locker room as Nick was coming in. A minute later he comes storming into my office dragging Nick with him and accuses him of stealing his sunglasses."

"I thought they were friends."

"Apparently not."

"What are you going to do?"

Billy shrugged. "Don't know. Nick says he didn't do it. Derek says he did and demands that Nick get fired."

"Don't you have to get rid of one of them soon?"

"Yeah, that's right, first of the year, I have to go down to one deputy."

"Well, doesn't that seem awfully *convenient?*"

"Lorry, I don't know what you're getting at, but I gotta go. I'll talk to you later. Bye. Oh! Love you!"

"Love you, too, Billy. Bye."

"Wow! That's big news! John might have killed Kasey's boyfriend?" Petra asked from the other room.

"You heard that?"

"Of course I heard it! You had the speaker phone on! Kasey next door probably heard it, too!"

"Well, I don't think John did it! John is—" but I didn't get to finish because the phone rang.

"Rutledge Historical Society, can I help you? . . . Oh, hi, Pamela. Aiden is okay, isn't he?. . . Oh, good. Yeah, sure. Got it. Go ahead. . . . All right, thank you, and if you see Aiden again, tell him I'll take care of it. . . . Bye."

"What was that?" asked Petra.

"Do you have to listen to all of my phone calls? I thought you were studying."

"Your phone calls seem to be getting more and more

interesting. Besides, I need a break." She walked in and stood behind my desk. "What was it?"

I held up the paper that I wrote on. "Aiden wanted me to get him these books."

"I thought he loved to go to the library?"

That made me chuckle. "That's what's funny about this. He does. But he wanted me to get his books so he could start working on the new exhibit! I'm glad I didn't officially find one when I was up there. He would have been seriously disappointed."

"That is funny. Well, go ahead now if you want to. I need a breather anyway."

"Okay, thanks, Petra."

With paper in hand, I walked over to the library, not knowing the surprise that awaited me there.

CHAPTER TWENTY-EIGHT

THE PUBLIC LIBRARY was on the corner of High Street and Bridge Street just down from the historical society, so it wasn't a long walk at all. It was one of the original buildings in Rutledge with the required red brick. But its architects went above and beyond. On the front of the building was an arched stained glass window of a frog reading a book. Let me tell you that frog caused more barroom brawls than any other thing in Rutledge. Why? They argued about what book the frog was reading. Yes, really. You wouldn't think that drunks even read books or cared what a frog might read. But that's just being judgmental, and I would never do that. Ahem. Well, maybe someday I won't. I'm still working on it.

I walked past the front patio with its redwood bench and patio table and entered the library. Catherin was behind the desk. She was not my favorite person, although Aiden pushed me to be kind to her, because as he put it *every human being has some redeeming value.* It was just so hard for me to relate to her. While it was true we were in the same age bracket—early thirties—she was so different from me. Take for instance our clothes: I wore stylish clothes with vivid colors, while Catherin wore drab long, dark skirts with almost matching dark drab blouses that were buttoned up to the top button.

She used to be the head librarian, but they had to replace her with Brandi, who was also weird, but tolerable, because Catherin was sick all the time. Again, Aiden told me to be more understanding, but it took so much effort to be understanding. If you are judgmental, it's just easy and requires no energy and no thought. Oh, wait.

"Hi, Catherin." Today she wore a long navy skirt with a dark red pinstripe. Her blouse was the same dark red as the stripe. At least she matched.

"Oh, hi, Lorry. Where's Aiden today?"

Hmmm. I didn't think she even liked him. Apparently I was being *way* too judgmental. Again. "He wanted me to pick up a couple of books. We're about to redo the exhibits, and he's excited about that."

"Oh, that is exciting! You'll find that everyone in town will want to come in to see what's new! I know I will." She noticed the paper in my hand. "What does he want today?"

I handed her the paper. "I don't know where he finds out about these books, but he has plenty on his list to read."

"These are over here."

Catherin walked toward the fiction section, and I followed because there was nothing better to do. But I was still upset about what Billy had told me about John. I don't know what possessed me, but I said, "Billy is going to bring Kasey's husband back in because someone saw him come out of the post office on the day of the murder."

Catherin, who had been moving her finger along book titles on a top shelf, turned toward me. "He *never* went into the post office! I saw him. He got to the corner"— she pointed out the window where she could see the corner clearly—"looked down toward the post office, but then turned around and ran back the way he had come —just like he always does."

"Ran? What do you mean 'ran'? That's what the anonymous caller said."

"Anonymous caller? That's bull pucky! He ran, just like he runs every single day before he goes in to work."

Nodding my head, I finally realized what she was saying. Sometimes, you know, I can be dense. "He's a runner! He wasn't running away from the post office, he was just running!"

"Exactly!" She nodded, turned back to the shelf, and pulled a book out. "Anonymous caller! Probably just some hoax or someone trying to get John into trouble."

I was liking Catherin more by the minute. Although I had never seen her so animated before, it suited her. And what great information she had given me! It might even get John off the hook for the murder—not that I ever thought he did it, though. The whole idea of it got me so excited that I turned and headed toward the door.

"Lorry! Aiden's books!" Catherin had found the second one by then and held them both up.

"Oh, yeah." I walked back to the desk so Catherin could check them out for me.

As I opened the door to the library, I waved the books in the air. "Thanks for the books, Catherin! And the information! Thanks so much for the information!"

Rushing out to the sidewalk, I could hardly wait to tell Billy about what I had just found out. And as I opened the door to the historical society, I realized that Aiden was right. Catherin had some redeeming value after all.

CHAPTER TWENTY-NINE

CALLING BILLY WAS the first thing on my mind, but it wasn't meant to be. Petra must have heard the door jingling when I came in, because as soon as Bingo and I closed the door, I heard Petra in the exhibit area.

"Ah, here's Lorry now to finish the tour for you."

After I told Bingo to stay by my desk, I walked to the back with a smile that I didn't feel plastered on my face. I didn't have time for this! I had to call Billy to clear John. But this was my job, and calling Billy would have to wait.

"Hello, everyone."

"I left off at the train, Lorry," said Petra as she hurriedly walked past me on her way to her desk.

That made me happy because there were just a couple of exhibits after that, so it wouldn't take me too long. But, as it turned out, Petra had started the tour backward, so I had to give them an almost complete explanation. It was a family of four, with a teenage boy and a preadolescent girl. Neither of the kids had a cell phone in their hands, and they actually seemed interested in the exhibits. They weren't wearing hiking clothes, either. All four of them wore what I would have to describe as *business casual*. It was nice to see people dressing up a little.

Since Petra hadn't even started with the train, I had to explain about it continually falling off the tracks and ending up in the canyon below. Then the family got into an animated discussion about taking the jeep trail from Rutledge to Sedona to search for some remnants of the old wreck. When I got them settled down from that, we continued to the rest of the exhibits. But all of them asked questions about each exhibit, and they didn't walk away until almost 11:30.

Then, just when I thought I was home free, the four of them strolled into the gift shop. Although I hadn't called Billy because I didn't want to with so many people around, I was just getting settled into my desk when they came out of the gift shop loaded with t-shirts, posters, and mugs that said *Rutledge Historical Society* on them. By the time they paid and left the building, it was 11:50.

"You're welcome," said Petra in a snotty voice after she heard the door close.

"Oh, sorry! Sorry! Thank you, Petra. Thank you very much. I'm sorry."

Without answering, she turned back to her computer, and I hurried to my desk. I had half the numbers tapped into the phone when the door jingled and opened and more people walked in.

"We want to see the new exhibits!" said the woman in the front. There were three of them, all young, all dressed in business attire. Then I realized it was lunchtime, and they wanted to spend theirs here. How awesome is that? Not. At least not now.

I did the only smart thing I could think of so I could call Billy. I tried to get rid of them. "I'm sorry," I said with a big smile, "but the new *exhibit* isn't done yet. Just the same old boring ones you've probably already seen a dozen times."

"Oh, we don't think they're boring! And we haven't been here in ages!" They pushed past me. "Come on, girls!" And they marched into the back.

Giving Petra an eye roll as I walked past her, I followed them to the back. But they were talking among themselves and didn't seem to need any assistance from me, so I returned to my desk.

As I walked by Petra, she said, "Lorry, it *is* your job." Before I had a chance to walk away, she added, "Job, from middle English *piece, article.*"

Sometimes she could act so juvenile, it was like she was sixteen years old. Oh, wait. She *was* sixteen years old. And she was right about it being my job. "Piece? Article? That doesn't even make sense."

She nodded. "That's what makes etymologies interesting. Regardless, it is your job."

I leaned over to whisper to her. "Yeah, I know it's my job, but *you're* the one who encouraged me to solve that guy's murder." Then I thought a minute. "Aren't you?" Sometimes I couldn't remember my own name. "Anyway, I have information to give Billy."

"Well, you can't call him with other people in here," she whispered. "That's just not right."

I gave her another eye roll for good measure. "I *know* that!" Then I stomped to my desk like I had something to be mad about—even though I knew I didn't.

Before the three young women had left, more people came through the door. Two couples came in, but it didn't look like they were together—I mean they didn't look like couples. They looked like four people who were acquaintances and nothing more. The man in front spoke up. "We'd like to see the new exhibits, please." They all wore business clothes. So far that day, except for the people that got the tour, there had been no tourists, just locals.

I was just about to give them my kindest go-away smile and tell them the same ole story, but the three women who had been in the back, took that moment to exit the building. One of them said, "No new exhibits yet, but the old ones are still cool! Toodle-loo!" And she and her friends stepped out the door, with the bell jingling behind them.

One of the new women wanted to leave when she learned there were no new exhibits, but the three others still wanted to stay, so they pulled her along behind them. I smiled an ingratiating smile and followed them as far as Petra's desk.

Leaning over, I whispered, "*What* is going on? Where are all these people coming from?"

She shrugged. "The new exhibit. It's usually up between Thanksgiving and Christmas."

"It's not even Thanksgiving yet! Besides, I thought you told me the first of the year!"

"Yeah, well, you have that long, but it's usually up earlier. And everyone in town knows it."

Throwing both hands into the air and my neck back, I said, "Whatever!" as I walked back to my office. No telling when I would get a chance to call Billy. I hoped John was okay and not on his way to Coyote Moon jail.

CHAPTER THIRTY

FINALLY, AN HOUR and a half later, there was a break in the constant stream of people. Several of them had left when I told them that the new exhibit wasn't up, but plenty of them piled into the back to look at the old exhibits again.

I tapped in Billy's number on the phone. When I got him, he said, "Listen, Lorry, I don't have time to talk; I have to leave for Coyote Moon."

Oh, no, I thought, he's hauling John off to jail. "John?"

"No, no, he's fine. I'll tell you tonight when I come over. I'll be there between six and six-thirty, and we can talk then. But I need to leave right now."

"Tonight's Aiden's karate class."

"Oh, that's right! Well, we'll work something out. See ya then. Gotta go. Love you."

I said I love you and bye and sat there stupefied. I had waited for hours to tell him, and now I didn't even get to say a thing. But at least he wasn't taking John into jail. Why was he going to Coyote Moon, anyway? Another suspect or something? I wouldn't find out for hours, if then.

Usually, as soon as Billy entered the house, Aiden spent every second with him. And on a karate night? They'd talk karate from the moment Billy came through the front door until they had returned from the lesson and Aiden was tucked safely into bed.

A few more people straggled in but walked through the exhibits quickly and left. I had just checked my email for the dozenth time when I glanced out the window to see a sheriff's car pull in front of the post office. That was curious, I thought. Billy was in Coyote Moon. When Derek got out of the car and walked in, I figured he was just checking his mail. Many of the people in Rutledge had post office boxes because for so long, several places in town had no mail delivery.

But when Derek came out a few minutes later with Zack, it confused me. At least this time, Zack didn't have handcuffs on and Derek even opened the front passenger door and let him in that way. Then he made a big U-turn and drove away.

Less than fifteen minutes later, the sheriff's car pulled up in front of the post office again and dropped Zack off. Zack got out of the front passenger door and waved when the car drove off. But he wasn't smiling, and when he walked back into the post office, his head was hanging down.

Before I had a chance to even process that, I heard Aiden skipping down the hallway. I heard him say hello to Petra as he skipped by, and then he skipped into my room and into my arms.

"Hi, Mommy!" He leaned down to hug Bingo. "Hi, Bingo!" Then he turned back to me. "Did you get my books?"

Smiling, I opened the drawer, pulled out his books, and handed them to him. "Thanks, Mom! Now I'm going to go upstairs to pick out the new exhibit." He slid off my lap, putting the books on my desk as he went. "You coming?"

"No, just let me know what you decide, and I'll help you bring everything down."

"Okay, Mommy! C'mon, Bingo!" Aiden skipped back down the hallway, and I heard him and Bingo race up the stairs.

It didn't take long for Aiden to go through the boxes and call down from the top of the stairs, "Mommy! I found one! Come help me with the box!"

"Lorry!" Petra shouted. "Aiden is ready for you to help him! Please do it, I need some quiet around here."

"I heard him, Petra. Thank you!" I didn't know what was going on with Petra this week. Usually, she revered the ground that Aiden walked on.

Walking to the stairs, I saw Aiden at the top. When he saw me, he started jumping up and down. "Hurry, Mom! Hurry!"

"So what did you pick out, Aiden?" I asked when I reached the top of the stairs.

"Well, I was between the constellations in an exhibit called *Stars over Rutledge* and another one about a murder here in the 50s. I chose the murder!"

"Murder? That's gruesome. Are you sure that's the one you want? I really like stars."

"I'm sure. I like stars, too, but a murder in Rutledge! How cool is that?"

That was a line straight out of Billy's mouth—or maybe mine. You have to be careful what you say around a kid. They pick it up quick. "All right, if that's what you

139

want."

The box with the murder exhibit in it was big and heavy. Two feet by three feet, it took both of us to pull and push it to the top of the stairs. "We got it this far, but how are we going to get it down the stairs? It's way too heavy. We could push it and hope for the best." I was joking, but Aiden took it to heart.

"No!" cried Aiden. "That will ruin some of the items inside—the pictures and stuff. And there's a gun!"

"A gun? There's a gun in the exhibit?" Shaking my head, I said, "Aiden, let's reconsider this."

"It will be locked up, Mom. You don't have to worry. And it's not loaded and there's no ammunition in the exhibit—except for the used bullet that killed the guy." He held up a plastic sandwich bag with a scrunched up piece of metal that hardly even resembled a bullet.

"How do you know the gun's not loaded?"

"I checked. Sheriff Billy taught me."

My hackles went up at that. Next time I saw Billy I would tell him a thing or two! Then I took a deep breath. Wait a minute. Aiden was a responsible kid. You hear about those kids finding their parent's guns and then accidentally shooting a friend or sibling. Billy—and his gun—was at the house all the time. It would be a good idea for Aiden to know if a gun was loaded or not. But—

Aiden must have heard me thinking, because he added, "I know I'm not supposed to pick up guns, but if one happens my way, now I know what to do with it. You know, Mom, how to make sure it's safe."

"You know you're never supposed to point a gun at anybody, even if you're sure it isn't loaded."

"Yes, Mommy, Sheriff Billy went through all that with me. No worries."

I sighed, shook my head, and said, "All right. All that is fine, but how are we going to get the box down?"

We both stood there trying to think while Bingo and Rocky were behind us smelling each other's butts. Then Aiden jumped up once. "I know! Remember that time Billy left the rope in the back of our car? We can use the rope to lower it down!"

I didn't remember why it was in there, although I did remember Billy putting it in there. But it was months ago. "He's probably already taken it out by now."

"Let's go check. C'mon!" And Aiden and Bingo pushed past me and ran down the stairs. When they got to the bottom, Aiden looked up at me. "C'mon, Mommy!" Then he and Bingo ran off.

I tromped down the stairs thinking it was an effort in futility, and then Aiden ran up to me jingling the car keys in his hand. "Let's go, Mom!" He and Bingo raced to the back door.

Following them out the back door, I opened the back, and just as Aiden remembered, there was a rope there. I shrugged and said, "You were right. It's still here. Now we have to figure out what to do with it."

CHAPTER THIRTY-ONE

THE THREE OF us trudged up the stairs—no, cancel that—I trudged up the stairs while it seemed like Aiden and Bingo took it in one giant leap. We tied the rope around the box in all directions to make sure it wouldn't slip out of the loop. And when we finished, surprisingly enough, we still had enough rope to lower it to the bottom of the stairs. What we didn't have, however, was the strength.

"Petra! We need you!" She had been such a grump lately that I didn't want to bother her, but it appeared we didn't have much of a choice. "Petra? Please? It will only take a minute." I wasn't sure how much she could help as she was a skinny sixteen-year-old who weighed about ninety-eight pounds. But we could use all the help we could get. Next, we would assign Rocky and Bingo to grab the end of the rope to help us pull.

"Please, Petra? We need you!" called Aiden in his sweetest voice.

"Oh, all right already! What do you need?" She stood at the bottom of the stairs and looked up.

"We need you up here to help us lower the box down

the stairs. It's really heavy."

"Here I come!" She lumbered up the steps like she had the weight of the world on her shoulders. I wondered what was wrong.

"I think if we all hold onto the rope, we can let it down easy and not break anything."

Petra pointed to the handrail. "See that brace that holds the handrail up? Let's wrap the rope around there first. It will give us more leverage in case the box gets away from us."

"Good idea," I agreed.

We did it, and the three of us slowly lowered the box to the bottom of the stairs. "Yay, Petra!" Aiden jumped up and gave her a high five. It was the first time I had seen her smile all week.

We all walked down the stairs, Petra first, and she stepped over the box onto the floor. "What's in this thing, anyway? What exhibit did you choose?"

"The murder!" said Aiden in a spooky voice.

Petra's eyes raised. "Oh! That exhibit has been hiding away up there for years. I've never seen it. That will bring the people in."

Oh, great, I thought as I rolled my eyes to no one except myself. But I didn't say it, because frankly, it wasn't nice. It was my job, and I chose it. But right now, with the murder of Kasey's boyfriend—I still got a funny feeling in my stomach when I thought that—I felt like I had other things that needed to be done rather than escorting people through do-it-yourself exhibits. Although in all fairness, most people did do it themselves, and usually the local business people did.

Petra started walking away and then she looked back. "Hey, you guys. You can't set up this exhibit until you get rid of one of the others."

"Oh, yeah," said Aiden. "We already picked out which one to go, though." He pointed to the exhibit at the end. "This one. Seasons of Rutledge. Kind of boring compared to a *murder!*"

"Well, good luck with all that," Petra said as she frowned and turned away.

After I helped Aiden push the box over to the side so it wouldn't be in anyone's way, I looked at Aiden and said, "Go upstairs and get that empty box up there so we can put the Seasons exhibit in it. I'll go get the keys to the exhibit case from Petra and be right back." I did need the keys, but I had a more important task to attend to.

When I got to her desk, she had already turned toward her computer and immersed herself in her studies. I put my hand on her shoulder. "Hey, Petra. What's goin' on? You've been really grumpy this week, and it's making me grumpy, too. Are you okay?"

She gave me a flat "fine," without turning around.

Then I remembered that I had been wanting to ask her something for a while now, but had kept forgetting. Billy had reminded me, too, but neither of us had remembered when Petra was around. "Hey, Petra. You and Mason want to come over next week for Thanksgiving?" Mason was her tattooed biker boyfriend. He was one of my first lessons in judging, because although he was tattooed, he was also a pre-med student in Flagstaff.

Petra turned her chair around so fast that I had to back up so our knees wouldn't clink together. "Really? Yeah, that would be so much better than staying at home waiting for, you know, *the drunk.*" She meant her father.

"Great! It's settled then. Can I have the keys to open

the exhibit area?" They were all behind heavy-duty unbreakable plastic. And locked.

"Sure." She dug into the bottom drawer of her desk and handed me the keys. "Oh." She sighed deeply and looked up at me. "You know, Mason and I really can't do that. It would leave my mom all alone with no one to eat with—because 99.9 percent my dad won't show up. Thanks for inviting us, but I guess we can't." Petra sighed again and returned to her computer.

In a moment of either brilliant inspiration or incredible stupidity, I'm still not sure which, I said, "You know, Petra, I've never met your mom. How 'bout if she comes, too?"

Another smile from Petra even bigger than the first graced her face. "Really? You'd have my mom, too?"

I nodded acting more confident than I felt. "Yes, of course. She is absolutely welcome in my home."

"All right! I'll tell her and let you know! That would be awesome!" Petra turned back to her computer and nodded her head enthusiastically.

What had I done? What would Billy say? Oh, there was no real need to worry about Billy. He took everything in stride. It was me who was the judgmental one. But I was working on it. Honest. I was working on it.

CHAPTER THIRTY-TWO

AFTER OPENING THE locked exhibit, Aiden and I
began dismantling it and putting everything in the box
he had brought downstairs. When the phone rang, I ran
to the front as best I could in my three-inch heels and
answered it. The caller wanted to know if the new
exhibit was up yet. I told her we were in the middle of
setting it up, and we would probably finish it just after
Thanksgiving. Since the box was so heavy, I figured it
might take awhile to get it set up.

When I hung up the phone, I checked my email.
There was one from Martha that surprised me. She said
she had a new project for me to work on, since she was
learning to type. I snorted and pushed away from the
computer almost sending me toppling into the fish tank
behind me. What? Martha is learning to type?

"Petra? Did you know Martha is learning to type?"

"Hugo's been threatening to buy her a how-to book
for years. Maybe he finally did."

"Hmmmph." I wondered what the new project was as
I guided my chair back to the computer. Martha said to
come over to the Town Offices to discuss it with her

when I got a chance. Putting my hands on the keyboard, I answered that I was busy right now with setting up the new exhibit and a lot more people coming in to look at it, but I would get over there when I could.

Then I returned to the back to find that all but the top part of the exhibit where Aiden couldn't reach was dismantled and in the box, the plastic—as far as he could reach—had been cleaned, and the bottom of the exhibit had been vacuumed. But at the present time, Bingo and Rocky were inside the exhibit with the front of it closed, and Aiden pointing at them and laughing.

It was funny. "Hey! I have an idea!" I opened the front of the exhibit and motioned Aiden to step inside. "Petra! Hey, Petra! Come and look at how well we fixed up the new exhibit! You'll love it!" Since I had lightened up her mood a little with the Thanksgiving invitation, I didn't think she'd give me one of her curt, sharp answers.

"Already? How'd that happen? I'll be right there."

I motioned for Aiden to be quiet, and then we both heard footsteps coming down the hallway. Aiden—I don't know where he gets this stuff—posed like Rodin's *The Thinker* or at least as close as he could get to it without a chair to sit on.

Petra strolled in, looked at the exhibit with Rocky, Bingo, and Aiden posing, and she nodded her head and said, "*That* is epic. Stay right there, Aiden. Lemme get my phone." And she hurried off and was back a few seconds later taking pictures of the "new" exhibit. "I gotta send these to Mason! He'll love this!" When she finished, she opened the front and invited the three characters out. "You still have to remove the rest of the Seasons exhibit, though," she said while pointing to the top of the exhibit.

147

"I couldn't reach those," said Aiden. "Mommy will have to take care of them."

"Yup, I'll get them."

I stepped into the exhibit to begin, but Petra said, "Not tonight, you guys, it's five o'clock! Time to go home!"

"Oh!" said Aiden, concerned. "I have karate tonight! I can't be late! Let's go, Mommy!"

I closed the front of the exhibit and walked to my desk to get my purse. As I walked by Petra's desk, she was straightening the papers on her desk. "See ya tomorrow, Petra. Thanks for your help today."

"See ya, Lorry," she said, turning to me with a bright smile. "I'll let you know about Thanksgiving."

Nodding, I followed Aiden and Bingo out to the car. I opened the back door for them, and they both jumped inside. Climbing in the front, I checked the rearview mirror to make sure that Aiden had his seat belt on, and I started the car and drove home.

After changing into something more comfortable, I made a chicken salad for dinner. On karate days, both Aiden and Billy wanted to eat light. Often when they returned from lessons, they would devour any leftover pizza that we had.

Aiden and I ate the salad, but he was anxious the whole time. Whenever he heard a car drive by or any kind of noise at all, he'd say, "Is that Sheriff Billy? He won't be late, will he?"

"I'm sure he'll be here in plenty of time, Aiden. Don't worry about it. Billy's never let you down yet, has he?"

"What if he doesn't make it back in time for my lesson? I can't miss! I'll fall too far behind the rest of the class."

148

"Billy says you're ahead of the rest of the class," I said.

Aiden sighed. "Yeah, but I still don't want to miss anything."

"I'm sure Billy will be here in time, but if he isn't, then I can take you."

"You? No, it has to be Sheriff Billy! You don't even know how to get there."

"Google maps, Aiden. But I'm sure he'll be here."

The conversation continued until Aiden had finished eating, and I sent him to his room to get his uniform on. "It's called a *gi*, Mommy," Aiden had told me a hundred times before, "and this is an *obi*," he said as he pointed to his yellow belt. The gi was made from white cotton and consisted of a loose white top and loose white trousers. The obi was a wide, thick belt made from cotton.

At 6:30, just as Aiden was about to drive me nuts with wondering if Billy would make it on time, Billy finally showed up. 6:30 is when they had to leave to get there in time. Aiden jumped into Billy's arms when he saw him and said, "C'mon, Sheriff Billy! We'll be late."

Billy had time to shrug, give me a quick kiss, and say, "We'll talk tonight when I bring him home."

I nodded, thinking that wasn't going to happen. Since I had spent such a restless night after we returned home from the haboob experience, I knew I needed to catch up on sleep tonight. Last night's dreams were of getting caught up in that wind and all the debris. I remember waking up and practically tasting dust in my mouth.

Although I wanted to stay up to talk to Billy about the events of the day, I fell asleep at 7:45 and didn't even wake up when he brought Aiden home and put him to bed.

CHAPTER THIRTY-THREE

I WOKE UP earlier than usual to find Bingo snuggled against my back. He was an amazing dog; he had an uncanny knack to know when either Aiden or I *needed* his company for the night. And if neither of us did, then he would take turns who he slept with. Bingo had slept with me two nights in a row—the haboob night and last night when I was still recovering. Tonight, no doubt, he would sleep with Aiden.

After letting him out the sliding glass door in my room, I put on my robe. It was too early to wake Aiden yet—or let him read—which is probably what he was doing. But I wasn't supposed to know about that. Of course I did, and he knew I did, but we both pretended otherwise. I waited a few minutes for Bingo to do his business, and then I opened the door and let him in.

Walking to the kitchen, I yawned. It had been a long night's sleep, but I needed it. And it was good that Aiden had been with Billy—whom I trusted unconditionally— so I didn't have to worry about him at all. Billy always did the right thing, and Aiden, although he was just seven, usually did the right thing too. Sometimes, he seemed so mature, it was like sharing a house with another adult.

On the kitchen table was a note from Billy that made me smile. *Hi, Darlin'. Sorry you're not still up, but I guess you needed the sleep. I'll stop by the historical society tomorrow morning so we can talk. Love you, Billy.* There were hearts all over it. He was so sweet! How did I ever come to deserve a great guy like Billy? Sometimes I wondered about that. My ex-husband Eddie was such an incredible jerk *and* a rotten guy, and it wasn't that many months ago that I was married to him. And now Billy. For whatever reason, someone as wonderful as Billy had come into my life. I know that I am and will always be grateful for it.

Aiden moseyed into the kitchen then, rubbing his eyes like he had just woken up. He wore his red feet pajamas I had special ordered from Maine. They had a picture of a moose head on the front with the words *I Love Moose* in big letters.

"Ready for breakfast?" I asked.

"Yeah, I guess so."

"The usual?" I offered to cook him eggs, oatmeal, anything he wanted, but he always wanted the same thing.

Aiden nodded, so I put a bowl in front of him, with the cereal and milk. Then I poured him a glass of orange juice with pulp. He liked that kind.

While he ate, I put a couple of eggs on to soft boil, and then put away the dishes in the dishwasher. When my eggs were done, Aiden had already finished and gone back to his room to get dressed. As I ate the eggs, I went over in my head what I wanted to talk to Billy about. It wasn't just what I had learned about John, but I was very curious about why Derek had picked up Zack and dropped him off again, and especially why Zack did not look happy about it even when he'd ridden in the front seat without handcuffs. That was so weird.

When I finished, I put the eggshells down the garbage disposer, washed off the plastic egg holder, and then showered and got dressed. Today was a beige slack suit with a brown blazer. I looked stunning, even if I did have to say so myself. But usually I didn't. Billy almost always told me how good I looked. That was another thing about him to feel grateful for. That, of course, and the fact that he *never* put me down compared to Eddie *always* putting me down.

Aiden jumped into my room wearing his *Rutledge Historical Society* sweatshirt and blue jeans. And his beloved Van's tennis shoes. Bingo followed him and was wearing his usual black, white, and tan coat, which was perfect if you were a Cavalier King Charles Spaniel.

"Let's go, Mom!" said Aiden. "The sooner we get to school, the sooner we can work on the new exhibit!"

I thought it was so cute how motivated Aiden was to finish the exhibit. His enthusiasm even affected me a little. As soon as I got in, I'd finish removing the Seasons of Rutledge exhibit so the space would be ready for Aiden when he finished his school day.

We got into the car, drove to the historical society, and parked. The three of us walked to Aiden's school, where he kissed me and Bingo and then skipped up to the stairs leading to the entrance of the school. His principal, Pamela Reilly, gave me a big smile and a wave. She was instrumental in my adopting Aiden, so I owed her a lot. But she was appreciative of me for discovering that Aiden could read when he had been stuck in remedial reading for who knows how many months. And I had discovered that not only could Aiden read, but he read at an adult level. Wasn't everybody surprised at that!

Bingo and I walked back to the historical society and found Billy's sheriff's car parked next to mine, but Billy wasn't anywhere in sight. I figured that Petra had let him in, so I retrieved my purse from the car. Then I opened the back door of the society and got the biggest surprise of my life.

CHAPTER THIRTY-FOUR

JUST INSIDE THE back door of the historical society was a makeshift closet with a ladder, a broom, Rocky's litter box, food and litter, and who knows what else. A long, dark curtain covered it. When Bingo and I stepped through the door, and I turned to make sure it was locked, I saw a big shape loom out of the closet. Suddenly its arms were around me holding me so tight that I couldn't move. I felt so scared that my knees went weak, and I almost peed my pants. Good thing my mama taught me always to go before I left the house. And now it was kissing my neck, and Bingo was barking his friendly *I want to play, too*, bark.

"Hello, beautiful," said Billy, releasing me.

"Billy! You scared me!" I turned around to see him with a big grin on his face. Although I briefly considered slapping him for scaring me like that, I didn't do it. Violence was not my style. So instead I kicked him in the knee. Whoa! Just kidding. I didn't do that either. What I really did was turn my back on him and stomp out of the room trying to control my anger—anger fueled by scared-to-death adrenalin running through my veins.

He caught up and tried to take my hand, but I pulled it away. "Lorry, don't be mad. I just want to take advantage of every minute I have to get my arms around you."

"Not like that, Billy. There's been two murders in this building, one behind this building, and now one across the street. And someone grabs me from behind like that? Not funny." When I walked by Petra's desk, I said, "Hi, Petra," but kept walking.

When I got to my desk, I plopped my purse down and crossed my arms. Billy gently turned me around to face him.

"Look, I'm sorry, Lorry. All of that is true. I just didn't think. I'm not perfect, you know. I promise I will never do it again." He held up three fingers in a boy-scout salute. "Come on, please? I'm sorry. It was wrong of me to do that."

Tears came into my eyes, and I threw my arms around his neck hugging him. Eddie, my ex-husband, in all the too-long years we were together, never, not even once, apologized. And he had plenty to apologize for, too. That Billy could do it so easily and so sincerely meant more than I could say. Well, that, and I was still trying to keep the adrenalin down. It might have been that, too.

"I love you, Lorry. I'd never deliberately do anything to hurt you. I'm sorry."

"I love you, too, Billy. And thank you for saying you're sorry. I appreciate that."

He pulled away from me, wiped the tears from my eyes without addressing it—which I also appreciated—and then said, "Now will you tell me what you wanted to tell me yesterday? It sounded important, but I had to leave to get to Coyote Moon."

"It was about John. I had information to clear him from the *phony* anonymous phone call."

"Ah, John's already cleared. That's why I had to go to Coyote Moon yesterday. Got the final report from the coroner. Time of death was 6:30 A.M. John *and* Kasey were both home then. The daycare center confirmed that Kasey dropped the baby off at 7:15, which gave Kasey time to drive to work, park the car, and then walk across the street to the post office. It would be stupid of her to kill the guy and then go back and *accidentally* find the body."

"I suppose, it could be said that she killed him at 6:30 and came back at 7:30 to wipe the prints off the gun."

Billy shook his head. "Yeah, that's true, but I found it very suspicious that there were no prints on the gun except for the one time Kasey picked it up. I wanted to drop the charges against her, but the prosecutor wouldn't let me. Fortunately, John is clear, though. But I'm curious, what did you find out?"

"Catherin at the library saw John stop at the corner, turn around and run the other way. She said he was running, because he runs every day. She said he looked down the street toward the post office, but never stepped a foot off the sidewalk on the other side of Bridge Street."

Billy nodded, looked away like he was thinking of something, and said, "Hmmm."

"That means the anonymous caller was just trying to put the blame on him."

"And take it off himself or herself. Yes, that's exactly what I was thinking."

"Speaking of blame—what happened with Nick and Derek?"

Billy looked away again. "I had to put Nick on administrative leave until there's an investigation."

"Investigation? You're the sheriff! What kind of investigation do you need?"

"Well, Derek's lock had been wiped clean of fingerprints, which was highly unusual. And his glasses *had* been found in Nick's locker. And Nick claimed he knew nothing about it. I had no choice."

"But it shouldn't take long to clear him, will it?"

"What makes you think he's innocent? Maybe he really did it."

Shaking my head, I said, "I don't think he's the type. And the sunglasses? What's so special about them, anyway?"

"Nothing, except they were Derek's. I don't know, Lorry." He looked at his watch. "I'm way late now, I gotta go." He leaned over and kissed me. "Love you."

"Love you, too, Billy," I said as he walked down the hallway. Then I remembered what else I wanted to ask him, so I hurried up and caught him before he got out the door. "Billy, why did Derek take Zack in again? Was there some question of his innocence?"

"I don't know anything about that."

"Well, it was weird, because Derek seemed to be really nice to him and even had him sit in the front seat of the car."

"Sheriff's car?" Billy asked.

"Yeah. It wasn't that long, and then he dropped Zack back off."

"I'm sure it's nothing, Lorry. They're probably friends."

"Friends? After Derek almost broke his arm last time he took him in? As the cliché goes, with friends like that,

157

who needs enemies?"

"If it didn't take that long, I'm sure it was something innocent. I wouldn't worry about Zack."

"I'm not worried about Zack," I said, but it made me think twice about everything that had gone on since the murder.

CHAPTER THIRTY-FIVE

THE BEST WAY to find out about Zack was to ask Zack himself. So I walked into where Petra was.

"Hey, Petra."

Today she wore a bright red dress and had bright red lipstick to match. She turned toward me with a smile on her face. The thought of not having to spend Thanksgiving at home lightened her burden considerably. It was good to see her feeling better and not so grumpy. I didn't need any help acting grumpy.

"Hi, Lorry. I asked my mom." Her smile faded briefly. "But I don't think she'll go. Her response was, 'What if your father comes home? What will he eat?' I told her that he hasn't come home for Thanksgiving for sixteen years. What makes her think he will now?"

"Billy knows your mom, doesn't he?"

"He knows her very well. She always came to get my dad out of jail when the jail was in town. Now Billy is nice enough to let the ole man stay in the holding cell instead of sending him to Coyote Moon—not that the ole man lets himself get caught so much anymore." She frowned and continued, "Anyway, yeah, Billy knows her.

Why?"

"How about if we ask Billy to talk to her? Maybe she'll listen to him."

The smile reappeared on her face. "Yeah! Great idea! I never thought of that! You want to, or should I?"

She said it in a way that told me she'd rather have me do it. "I'd be happy to do that, Petra. No problem.

"Hey, listen, I'm going to run across the street to talk to Zack, but I'll put the sign on the door so no one bothers you. Okay?"

Petra raised her eyebrows. "Oh, I don't think there will be anybody here until after Thanksgiving."

"Why would you say that? They were piling in yesterday."

Petra rummaged through her backpack, pulled out the weekly *Rutledge Chronicle*, and handed it to me. Right on the front page was the picture she had taken of Aiden, Bingo, and Rocky in the exhibit with a note under the picture that said *The new exhibit will be available for viewing after Thanksgiving. (But this isn't it!)*

I laughed when I saw it. You couldn't see Aiden's face, but you could see him in full form. "Aiden will love this! When did you get it to them?"

"I didn't. I told Mason what was going on and sent him the picture. He figured if there were an official announcement that the new exhibit wasn't open yet that people wouldn't bother us so much."

Looking up, I said, "Thank you, Mason." The reason I looked up is because Mason was north of us, and north is up, right? Well, isn't it?

"So, anyway, no need to put the sign up. I don't think I'll be bothered."

"Gotcha. Thanks." I turned and walked out the front

door, hearing it jingle as I closed it behind me.

A minute later I walked into the Rutledge Post Office. Taking a quick tour of the post office boxes, I didn't see Zack anywhere around, so I knocked on the door marked *Private Employees Only*. And that made me wonder about the difference between a private employee and a public employee. But no matter, a second later Zack peeked out the door with a broom in his hand.

"Hi, Lorry!" He gave me a warm smile.

I smiled back and reached out and gave his shoulder a warm squeeze. I liked this kid. "Listen, Zack, can I ask you a couple of questions? Alone?"

He pulled me into the room. "They're all up front helping customers. And someone is putting mail in boxes on the far side. No one can hear. What's up, Lorry?"

"Yesterday. What went on between you and Derek?" Before he could answer, I added, "This is between you and me."

Zack nodded, looked down, then abruptly looked up at me. "He didn't hurt me this time."

"I saw that. But I want to know what he did. Why did he take you in?"

"Oh, he didn't take me in. We just drove around for a few minutes."

"But why, Zack? What are you holding back?"

"He wanted to talk—about what happened the day of the murder." Zack looked down again. "Well, basically he wanted to know my alibi again. Which I didn't understand because I had already given all that information to Billy, and I figured Derek would have access to it, too."

"What is your alibi?"

He shrugged. "I paid my rent right before I came into

161

work. And as soon as I told that to Derek and explained why the landlady would remember that—I offered to help her move some furniture when I got home—he drove me back here. But—" He started but hesitated.

"What is it, Zack?"

"I felt like there was, you know, an ulterior motive or something. Like he wanted to set me up, so he needed all the facts before he attempted it."

"Thank you for telling me, Zack."

He put his hand on my arm. "Don't tell Billy, okay? I don't want to get Derek into any trouble. I don't think that would be good for me at all."

Nodding, I said, "I think you're right about that, Zack. I definitely think you're right about that."

CHAPTER THIRTY-SIX

IT WAS SUCH a beautiful day—blue sky, cool but not cold, a gentle breeze—that I thought of walking over to the Town Offices to see Martha, but I decided to drive instead. Striding back into the historical society accompanied by the jingle of the bell, I told Petra where I was off to and then slipped out the back door, giving a dirty look to the curtained closet as I went by.

The drive to the Town Offices took only a minute. I parked in the back of the modern pink and gray concrete building. As I followed the path, I walked by the large ornamental rock and the sign with the Rutledge seal on it, which showed a baby javelina. Although I thought it was cute with a slight smile on its face, you wouldn't believe all the ruckus it caused not only when it was first adopted but occasionally since then. The people against it had all kinds of reasons such as: they're ugly, they stink (as if you could smell them from the sign), they're feral, and they're common. Really? Common? Sounds like someone was feeling a little hoity-toity that day.

Opening the door, I walked past the waiting area with

all the magazines and strode up to the receptionist who was safe behind glass—safe probably because of people who spent too long waiting at the DMV—and asked to see Martha. I knew where her office was because I had been here so often, but, you know, propriety calls.

The receptionist directed me down the hallway lined with pictures of different varieties of Arizona cactus. When I walked into Martha's office, she smiled warmly at me. I loved her office. With its pale tones of gray and brown, I always felt at home here. And I remembered the first time I saw those pictures of wild horses running and thought it meant you were coming into money. And I did! So maybe it works! So I looked at them again. You know, you can't be too thin or too rich. Oh, wait.

"Hi, Lorry. So good to see you."

"Good to see you, too, Martha." Aiden and I had stayed at Martha and her husband Hugo's bed and breakfast before we moved into our house. They were like grandparents to Aiden. He loved them. And I thought they were awesome, as well.

She cleared her throat like she felt embarrassed. "Well, um, you've probably heard the rumor that I'm trying to learn to type." When I nodded, she continued. "Look at this! Hugo got it for me. My own laptop. I'm doing pretty good, too. I know almost all my letters now, and I only have to look at the keys occasionally.

"What I'm trying to tell you, Lorry—"

"Please don't tell me you're going to let me go, Martha." My heart fell into my stomach at the possibility. The life of nothing to do but golf and country clubs wasn't for me.

"Let you go? Oh, don't be silly, Lorry. Remember, I told you—or told Petra to tell you, I can't remember now

—that I had a new project for you."

Relieved, I gushed, "Oh, that's right. Thank goodness! I was afraid there for a minute I'd have to learn to play golf!"

That made Martha laugh. "No such luck, Lorry Lockharte. There's your new project over there." She pointed to a big box leaning up against the wall. It said *Scanner* on it.

Having never used one before, I said, "What's it do?"

"You know all those boxes of documents and pictures upstairs in the historical society? I want you to scan every single document and picture up there. And you'll need to organize them into files, but I know you're good at that sort of thing." She pointed to the box. "I bought one that can do slides, too, because I think I remember some of those up there in those boxes. You'll have your hands full for a while. I don't think you need to worry about job security."

Nodding, I said, "Yeah, you're right. I hope I can finish before I get to retirement age!"

That made Martha laugh again. "I'm sure it will be more interesting than editing and typing my dry letters and documents." Looking at the box, she said, "Oh, do you think you can get it, or should I have called Billy to bring it over to you?"

I knelt down and picked up the box. It wasn't that heavy, maybe twenty pounds. But it was bulky. It was more than two feet across on one side and almost that on the other side. Almost a foot deep. "I can handle it, Martha. But I'll probably get Billy to carry it upstairs for me!"

"And I've ordered a new computer to hook it up to and a new computer desk to go with it. And a table for the scanner."

"Thanks, Martha. Just point me toward the door." I could see over the top of the box, but just barely.

"Oh, Lorry. That's why I love you. You always make me laugh. Can you get someone to set everything up for you, or should I arrange it?"

"How about Zack? That's what he's taking in college now." When Martha nodded, I asked, "Can I pay him?"

"Yes, of course. Just send me an invoice for him."

I felt happy about that, but it didn't matter, because had she said no, I would have paid him out of my own pocket. And I had deep pockets. "All right. Bye, Martha. Thanks!"

As I was about to step through the door, Martha called me back. "Lorry, how's the new exhibit coming?"

"You mean you didn't see Aiden's picture on the front page?"

"Front page?"

"*The Rutledge Chronicle.*"

"They have one at the front. I'll have to check it out."

"Anyway, Aiden has picked out a new exhibit, and I'll finish taking down the old one today. Aiden is so excited about putting up the new exhibit! He can't wait."

"Which one did he choose?"

"The murder in Rutledge."

"Ooohhhh." She said nothing but looked concerned.

"Should I have him change it?"

"No, no. That one has had a rest for many years. Maybe this is the time to break it out again. It was a murder that was never solved."

She sighed and continued, "Anyway, thanks, Lorry. The company will deliver the computer and accessories early next week." Martha stood up, took something off her desk, handed me a manila envelope, and shrugged. "There's quite a few in here. I've been saving them up thinking I could do them myself." She shrugged again, looking embarrassed. "Do you mind doing a little more typing until I get better at it?"

She slid it between my hand and the box, and I grasped it with my thumb. "No problem, Martha. Bye."

"Bye, now."

As I walked down the hall past the cactus pictures, I realized that I had forgotten to ask her something, so I turned around and came back. "Martha, would you and Hugo like to come for Thanksgiving?"

"Oh, sorry! I meant to ask if you and Billy would like to come to our house. We're expecting a full house of guests for that whole weekend."

"Okay, we'll miss you, but I understand. Bye!"

On my way out, the receptionist reading the newspaper she was bringing to Martha almost ran into me. But I managed not to stumble, and then I backed my way out the front door. After smiling and winking at the cute javelina sign, I continued to my car. I stuffed the big box into the back and drove back to the historical society.

CHAPTER THIRTY-SEVEN

LEAVING THE BOX in the car, I walked into the back of the historical society and called out, "Honey, I'm home," as I walked through the hallway.

"Who you talkin' to? Billy's not here." Petra turned her chair to look at me.

I walked up to her desk and said, "I'm talking to you!" I reached out to pinch her cheek, but she batted my hand away.

She looked at me with eyebrows raised and hope in her eyes. "Have you asked Billy yet? You know, about my mom?"

"No, I haven't had a chance since we talked about that. I'll talk to him tonight if not before."

"Okay." She turned back to the computer, but I could tell she was disappointed.

As soon as I reached my desk, I realized that I had left the envelope with Martha's documents in the car along with the box. Billy could carry the box in sometime, but I needed the envelope now. Walking past the remnants of the Seasons of Rutledge exhibit, I remembered that I needed to get the rest of the exhibit taken down so Aiden could start on the new one when he returned after school today. I hurried to the car, retrieved the envelope, hurried back to my desk, and looked at the documents. They needed a lot of editing, and that would take a while, so I got out my green pen and got started.

When I finished typing the first very long document, I decided that since all the documents were long, I would send them to Martha as I finished them. So I attached the document to an email and sent it off. I did that to the second and third one also. But after I finished the third one, I happened to look at my watch and realize that Aiden would arrive in just a few minutes. Setting the last two documents aside, I hurried into the back room to finish removing Seasons of Rutledge from the exhibit area.

I had just put several items into the box, and I was reaching for the others when I heard the back door open, and I knew Aiden had arrived. Unfortunately, I was just a few minutes late.

He walked around the corner and saw me there. The look of disappointment on his face didn't get past me.

"I'm sorry, Aiden. I had a really busy day. I'll be finished in a sec."

Looking up at me taking the final items off the exhibit wall, he said, "You don't like doing it. I thought you liked it like I did."

"Oh, I don't mind doing it, Aiden, but I don't like it as much as you do. But that's okay. We can put up the next one together."

Aiden looked away, kicked a piece of lint on the floor, and bent down to pet Bingo. "That's okay, Mommy. I'll do the bottom and then you can do the top."

I climbed out of the exhibit, transferred the items

from my arms into the box, and knelt down beside him. "That sounds great! We can do the top together. You tell me where you want everything, and I'll put it up there for you. Okay?"

He nodded, but his heart wasn't in it. I felt like I had taken the joy of doing the project away from him. After hugging him, I walked back to my desk to finish the documents for Martha. Bingo ran up the stairs, probably hoping to cuddle with Rocky.

I finished one more document and sent it off to Martha. Then I stood up and walked to Petra's desk. Holding my hand to my lips for Petra's benefit, I stood there and listened. Aiden was walking back and forth from the box with the murder stuff in it to the exhibit. He was softly singing to himself. Although I couldn't hear what song it was, I figured that he must be back to his happy self if he was singing. So I went back to my desk feeling much more relieved. His happiness made me feel so good, that I almost started singing myself.

The last document was shorter, so I was drawing close to the end when I heard a crash from the back. I thought maybe Aiden had dropped something, and that he would pick it up and go on with his work. But I should have known better. The crash was too loud for that. A second later, he screamed from the back, "Mommy! Mommy!" I heard Bingo's feet running down the stairs.

When I reached Aiden a second later—I swear my feet didn't hit the floor on my way back to my son—he was lying on the floor, sobbing, with a step ladder beside him that he must have dragged from the back and fallen from. His left forearm was twisted at an unnatural angle. Bingo was snuggled up next to him whining softly.

"Mommy, it hurts. It really hurts!"

"Oh, Aiden." My heart was in my mouth. I knelt down beside him to comfort him and yelled to Petra to call Billy that we needed a ride to the hospital. Tears were streaming down my face and streaming down his face.

Aiden looked up at me and said, "Mommy, it's okay. Don't be sad. I'm sure I'll be okay." Then he sniffled and continued, "After it stops hurting and all."

I wanted to hug him to me, but I was afraid to touch him at all. "Does anything else hurt, son? Or just your arm? Did you hit your head?" It's difficult to be pragmatic when you're panicked.

"No, Mommy. I landed on my arm. It's the only thing that hurts." He looked up at me with his eyes still full of tears. "A lot."

"I'm sorry, Aiden. I'm so sorry." I ran my hand across the top of his head, ruffling his hair. "I was going to do the top. Why didn't you wait for me?"

He sniffed. "Because I knew you didn't really want to do it, and you were just doing it because I wanted you to."

Didn't that make me feel like the bad mom of the month. "I'm sorry, honey. I was going to do it though." I wasn't going to lie to him—I was doing it because he wanted me to.

"It's okay, Mommy. I still love you. And when I get well, we can finish together."

It was so sweet of him to give me another chance. That was who Aiden was. He had a huge heart, and I knew how lucky I was to have him as my son.

"Lorry"—Petra walked over to us, knelt down, and stroked Aiden's hair—"Billy says he'll be here in five minutes."

Although I felt furious, I didn't want Aiden to see it, so I kept any snide comments to myself about Billy taking five minutes to arrive. The sheriff's station was one minute away. Didn't he realize if I asked him to take Aiden to the hospital that it needed to be immediately?

CHAPTER THIRTY-EIGHT

BILLY CAME RUNNING in a few minutes later with a look of dread on his face. Petra had already returned to her desk, and Billy knelt down beside Aiden. "You all right, little pard?"

I was still mad at him for taking five minutes, and when he asked that I wanted to scream "No, he's not all right! Look at his arm!" But I kept quiet and let Aiden answer.

"It hurts, Sheriff Billy. It hurts bad."

"Just your arm, though? Nothing else hurts? You didn't hit your head?"

"No, just the arm, I landed on it. Mommy already asked me all those questions. Let's go."

Billy smiled at me and must have taken my sour expression to be worry over Aiden, which it partially was. Then he turned back to Aiden. "Okay, little pard. Let's scoop you up and put you in the truck."

The truck, I wondered. When I followed Billy and Aiden to the front and saw Billy's big truck with a full back seat, I figured out why Billy took five minutes to get there. He had gone home to swap the sheriff's car with

173

his truck. And I felt horrible. Color me ashamed. Very, very ashamed.

The back seat of his sheriff's car was hard plastic and extremely uncomfortable. And I can unfortunately attest to that. Billy didn't want Aiden to be uncomfortable for his trip to the hospital. I should have known that Billy would always put Aiden's best interests first. Grabbing my purse out of my desk, I slipped the leash on Bingo and followed Billy and Aiden out the door.

The truck had a red flashing light on top with a cable that went through the driver's side window. On the side of the truck, was a magnetic sign with the Rutledge town seal on it—the one with the baby javelina—and a gold star overlaid on top of it. Beneath it, in thick black letters, it said *Sheriff*.

Billy got to the truck and opened the door while still holding onto Aiden. And then he gently put him down on the seat. "Listen, little pard. I'm going to drive there really fast, so we can get the doctor to stop the hurting. So I'd like to put the seat belt on you. I won't put it on your sore arm, though, is that okay?"

Aiden nodded and said, "Yes, Sheriff Billy," all while tears slid down his face.

Billy opened the front door for me and ran to the other side of the truck. I lifted Bingo into the seat, but then closed the door, ran to the other side with Billy, opened the back door and slid in next to Aiden.

"Not too close, Mommy. Don't touch my arm."

"I won't, sweetie, don't worry." After moving away from him enough so I wasn't touching his arm, I put my arm around him. Then I put my lips to his head and kissed him. "You know I love you, baby, right?"

"I know, Mommy."

By this time, Billy had turned the siren on and had already crossed the bridge from Rutledge to Coyote Moon, and we were tearing down Broadway at a frightening pace. Wasn't I glad that I wasn't in the front seat having to watch the close calls. But I did look up just in time to see Billy swerve around some jerk talking on his cell phone and not paying attention to the red light and siren. I closed my eyes and buried my face in Aiden's hair, making sure not to get too close and hurt his already hurt arm.

The hospital in Coyote Moon was in the center of town. Although it had started out at the edge of town, the town had spread out around it. It was a large four-story brick building. Billy pulled up in front of the emergency room entrance and jumped out of the car, leaving the siren and red light blazing. He ran to Aiden's door, opened it, and pulled Aiden out, holding him in his arms.

"You don't have to carry me, Sheriff Billy. I can walk by myself."

"I *get* to carry you, little pard."

"What about Bingo?"

"He'll be fine in the truck. I'll leave the windows partially open, and it's cool out. Plus, after I drop you off in there, I'll come back out and park in the shade, just in case."

By that time, I had gotten out and come around the truck, so the three of us hurried toward the emergency room doors. There was a large red sign that said *Flu Alert! If you have a cold or flu symptoms, please ask for a mask.* I hoped that we all didn't come down with the flu just from being there. The doors slid open—so we didn't have to touch anything—and we walked in.

175

Billy gently eased Aiden onto a chair in the waiting area and told me he was going to park and would be right back. I kissed Aiden on the forehead, told him I'd be right back, and approached the reception desk. No one was there. What if I was having a friggin' heart attack? Turning, I looked at Aiden. He shrugged, and I tried to ignore the tears still seeping out of his eyes.

While looking at the other people sitting in the waiting room, I wondered how soon they would take Aiden. One man in his twenties appeared to have a broken nose that was bleeding. He had a grocery bag full of red tissues and a roll of toilet paper next to him. He would probably be next, and it made me wonder who they would take before a bleeder who had been bleeding for a while. There was a middle-aged woman, alone, at the other end of the waiting room who had one of those masks on. I'm glad she wasn't on our side of the room.

There was a line of weird-looking wheelchairs lined up outside the nurses' station. They were tall, red and black, and had a tank of oxygen on a shelf underneath them. One of them had a sign on it that said *Try me*. On the other side of the room was a large vending machine with all kinds of snacks inside. Next to it was a stand with a coffee machine and white styrofoam cups. Next to that was an industrial-sized wastebasket with a gray liner folded over the sides, and beside that were two drinking fountains in different heights. Across from the reception desk was the security desk. It had a coat rack behind it and one of those plastic glove dispensers on the wall. The idea that a security guard would need plastic gloves grossed me out. Aforementioned security guard nodded at me when I looked at him.

A minute later, a tired-looking nurse appeared, and I

pointed to Aiden. Billy was sitting next to him now. I didn't even notice him come in. The nurse took all my insurance information and asked me to bring Aiden up to her. Billy helped him get up, and then Aiden walked over. She took his pulse and his blood pressure, looked but didn't touch his arm, and then told us it wouldn't be that long. While we were up at the desk, the bleeding man had gone in to see the doctor. He left his grocery bag of bloody tissues beside the seat where he had been sitting.

Aiden and I sat down by Billy, who looked at me and asked, "How long did they say it would be?"

"She said not long. So unless someone comes in with chest pains, I imagine that Aiden will be next."

"It's lucky there aren't many people in here. I've been in this waiting room before when it was packed. Can you wait, little pard?" Billy asked Aiden.

Aiden nodded but didn't say anything. His tears had mostly dried, but a stray one slipped down his face now and then. I stood up, walked to the vending machine, and reached inside my purse. I took out a few single dollar bills and bought two packages of M&Ms. Aiden loved them. When I reached him, and he saw what I had, he gave me a big smile.

"Thanks, Mommy." He took them and tore one open with his mouth. "Sheriff Billy says I'll probably need an X-ray."

"I'm sure you will, son," I answered.

"Will it hurt?"

"Not a bit. And maybe the doctor will let Billy 'n me stay with you while they take it."

A nurse came out of the double doors at the far end of the room with a chart in her hands. "Aiden

Lockharte!"

Billy and I both stood up, and Billy helped Aiden to his feet. "Let's go."

CHAPTER THIRTY-NINE

AS WE WALKED toward the nurse and the open door, I saw a big sign that said *Coyote Moon Silent Witness.* It showed a stack of money and said "Tipsters could earn cash rewards up to a thousand dollars." Apparently you can make big bucks being a professional tattletale. But since Coyote Moon had grown so big with the casino and all, the crime in the city had grown along with its size. Someone told me that there were even gangs starting to show up. So I guess they needed things like Silent Witness to help them solve the crimes.

The three of us followed the nurse into the back area where there was a U-shaped desk that took up most of the large room. There were several people dressed in hospital garb doing various things at the desk. Across from the desk were several examining rooms, most of them with their bland-colored curtains drawn. We turned a corner, and the nurse indicated the room with the open curtain.

Billy lifted Aiden onto the table, and the nurse said the doctor would be right in. Then she strode out through the door and pulled the curtain closed behind her.

179

"Right in" turned out to be more than twenty minutes later.

"I'm Dr. Adams," he announced as he walked in. He was middle-aged, serious, and in a hurry. After a brief nod to me and Billy, he walked up to Aiden. "What do we have here? That doesn't look like a regular arm should look, does it?"

"I think I broke it," said Aiden.

"I think so, too. But how about if I take a closer look? I'll need to cut your sweatshirt off, though." Dr. Adams pulled a heavy-duty scissors out of a drawer.

"No!" said Aiden. "It's my favorite shirt!"

"We can get you another one just like it, Aiden," I said.

"No, I like *this* one. And it's broken in just like I like it."

Dr. Adams put the scissors down and stepped back up to Aiden. "I can try to pull it over your head, but it might hurt your arm. Do you still want me to try?"

"Yes, but try to be careful and not hurt my arm. I really like this sweatshirt—it's where my mommy works —and I want to keep it." It was the Rutledge Historical Society sweatshirt he had put on that morning.

"All right. Here we go."

As much of a hurry that I thought the doctor was in, he went exceedingly slow with Aiden's sweatshirt until he got it over his head. He had started with removing Aiden's right arm, which wasn't injured, and then he focused on gently getting the left arm out of the sleeve. He did a great job, and Aiden was even smiling when he finished.

"It didn't hurt! Thank you for doing that, doctor!"

The doctor bowed to him. With Aiden sitting there

with no shirt on, the doctor carefully put a hospital gown on him and with the arm sticking out of the sleeve, the doctor said, "Yup, it sure looks like it's broken. Let's get an X-ray to see just how serious a break it is." He turned to me and Billy. "I'll send someone in to take him to X-ray. You're both welcome to tag along." And just like that he was gone and making me wonder if I had waited so long that I had imagined the whole thing.

A few minutes later an X-ray technician came into the room. She announced that she was taking Aiden to X-ray and that we could follow. Then she undid the brakes on the table where Aiden was sitting, asked him to lie down, and then pushed him out of the room and down the hallway with us following. Through the entire walk including the turns and other hallways, the nurse never stopped talking. I swear she was worse than Kasey—well, how Kasey used to be, anyway.

We arrived at the X-ray room, and she moved Aiden from the table she brought him in on to the table under the X-ray machine. He looked at me with fear in his eyes. "Are you sure it won't hurt, Mommy?"

I leaned down and kissed him on the forehead. "Yes, sweetie, I am positive. I've had a few X-rays in my life, and they don't hurt at all. And they're quick! It will be over before you know it. You stay real still so they only have to do it once, okay?" Aiden just nodded.

The nurse adjusted Aiden's position, put his arm out just so, and brought the machine down close to it. "Let's go behind the screen now, please," she said to me and Billy.

The "screen" as she called it, was a large piece of heavy-duty glass or plastic that apparently blocked out the radiation from the X-rays. "Okay, Aiden, don't move, and hold your breath until I tell you to let it go." She pushed a button, and the machine made a small noise. Then she told Aiden he could breathe, and she walked out and adjusted Aiden and his arm to a new position. She did that three times and then said, "Okay, Aiden, all done now. Let's get you back to your room." She moved him back to the other table and started pushing the table with Aiden on it back to the examining room.

Aiden tried to move around so he could look at me, but the nurse told him to lie still. I think he wanted to talk to me, and she didn't want him to because she wanted to do all the talking. Her talking never stopped until we were back in the room with the brakes set, and then she left the room.

Billy helped Aiden to sit up, and Aiden said, "You were right, Mommy. It didn't hurt. What's next?"

"The doctor will come back in after he looks at your X-rays and will tell you the next step," explained Billy. "If it's a simple break, then he can fix it today and put your arm in a cast."

Aiden nodded and didn't ask what happened if it wasn't a simple break, so I didn't either. I was hoping that Billy would lean over and tell me, but it was a small room, and he couldn't have done that without Aiden hearing. What I thought a complicated break required was surgery, but I hoped that wasn't the case. Since the bone wasn't sticking through Aiden's skin, thank goodness, maybe this would be just simple. I hoped so—I hated to see my boy going through this.

The tears on Aiden's face had dried, and there were no fresh ones—probably because the excitement of the waiting room and seeing the doctor had taken his mind off the pain of his broken arm. The three of us talked about where we would go for dinner, and Aiden said he was tired and didn't care. I suggested a drive-thru burger joint so we could get home quickly, and it was unanimous. Then all we had to do was wait for the doctor to see what the prognosis would be. It seemed like it was taking way too long.

CHAPTER FORTY

MANY MINUTES LATER, the curtain moved and Dr. Adams appeared carrying an X-ray in his hand. He put it up on the wall and turned on the light behind it.

Then he faced us and said, "Aiden has a displaced fracture of both the radius and ulna." He pointed to the breaks on the X-ray. "See here, where the bones aren't lined up? That makes it displaced and means I have to put them back into place."

Frowning, I asked, "Does that mean surgery then?" I heard Aiden groan beside me.

"No, not at all. Since it's a *closed reduction*, it's routine, and I can do it right here and then put the cast on." He turned toward Aiden and ruffled his hair. "You'll be all set to go, young man!"

That was kind of the doctor to do that. I liked him better already.

"What's a cast?" asked Aiden.

"It's like a big, hard bandage that keeps the bone from moving out of place. But first, I have to get the bone put back into place. So I'm going to put something in your arm that will take the pain away and make you feel sleepy. All right? Let's get started now." He started walking toward the curtain, but Aiden stopped him.

"Is it going to hurt?"

The doctor turned back and put his hand on Aiden's shoulder. "I'm not the kind of doctor who says it doesn't hurt when it does. When the needle goes into your arm, it will hurt a little. But after the medication goes in, then what I do to your arm shouldn't hurt at all. If it does, you tell me right away, and I'll make it right. Okay? Is that a deal?" He stuck out his hand to shake Aiden's and then exited the room.

Aiden shook his hand and gave the doctor a half smile. But I could see he was scared, and that tears had started rolling down his cheeks again. I looked at Billy hoping he could offer some words of advice or something, anything, to make Aiden feel better.

He stepped up to Aiden. "Little pard," he said, "let me ask you this. Did your brothers ever pinch you when you were in foster care?"

"Yes, and it hurt!"

"How much?"

Aiden shrugged. "Not that much."

"Well, depending on how hard they pinched you, the needle going into your arm will hurt less."

"Really? It won't hurt any more than a pinch?"

Billy shook his head. "Nope."

Aiden breathed out a long sigh and visibly relaxed. "All right then. I can take it."

Billy put his arm around him and said in a confidential voice that I could still hear, "Listen, Aiden. This is important. You don't have to be tough to be a man. It's okay not to be tough. It's okay to cry. Men cry. It's okay."

In that moment, I wanted to grab Billy up and drag him to the nearest altar to marry me. That—a man who could say that and believe it—was exactly the kind of man I wanted to marry. I wanted *that* man. I wanted Billy. But the scene before me was so sweet that I didn't say a thing.

Aiden said, "Thank you, Sheriff Billy. I'll cry if I want to then and not be ashamed."

"No need to be ashamed of crying, Aiden. Never be ashamed of that. It means you're human—and definitely *not* less of a man."

The nurse came in at that poignant moment and spoiled it for me. I sighed deeply and then tried to focus on what was going on, because she had brought with her an IV setup, and she was getting the needle ready to stick Aiden.

"Aiden, sweetie, are you ready for this?"

He looked at Billy. "It will only hurt as much as a pinch, right, Sheriff Billy?"

"That's all. I can show you if you want." Billy held his thumb and forefinger out and moved it toward Aiden's leg.

Aiden laughed. "No, no, that's okay. I'll take your word for it."

"What I could do," said Billy, "is pinch your leg at the exact moment she puts the needle in. Then you won't know where the pain is coming from. What do ya think?"

"I think I'll be fine with just the needle."

"Are you sure? 'Cause I think this is a great idea!" He moved his thumb and forefinger close to Aiden again, and Aiden pushed it away.

"I'll be fine, I'm sure."

186

After the nurse had set up the IV equipment, she stood by Aiden with a needle in her hand. "Are you ready?"

He nodded, but a couple of tears slipped out of his eyes. "Yes."

As she slid the needle in, Billy came toward Aiden with his thumb and forefinger outstretched, which made Aiden laugh. Then the nurse said, "All done."

Aiden looked at the needle still in his arm and grew pale. "You left it there," he said helplessly.

"Yes, Aiden. It needs to stay there while the doctor works on your broken arm." She held up another needle filled with fluid. "And this will help even more." She put the needle into the IV device and pushed the plunger.

Aiden felt the effect almost immediately. The stiffness in his body from being scared melted away. He nodded and closed his eyes.

But even Aiden did better than I did. I almost fell over until Billy caught me. Then the doctor came in and started working on Aiden, but I stayed in Billy's arms with my face buried in his neck. Aiden didn't make a sound. I didn't look. Then Billy said, "It's okay now, Lorry. The doctor has straightened the arm and is now putting the cast on. It's interesting. Take a look."

But I couldn't, so Billy gave me a play-by-play. "He put like a stockinette mostly over where the arm was broken. Now he's wrapping cotton padding all over it."

"Aiden? Can you hear me?" the doctor asked.

Aiden sighed. "Yeaaah." He sounded sleepy. It made me feel good just to hear his voice.

"What color cast would you like?"

"I like blue."

"All right."

"Now the doctor picked up a roll of blue fiberglass," said Billy. "He put it in some kind of liquid."

"It's just water," said the doctor.

"Thanks," said Billy, then he continued describing to me what was going on. "He took it out of the water and is wrapping it around Aiden's arm." Billy pushed me gently away from him. "Come on, Lorry, take a look."

I looked and Aiden had a cast from his hand all the way past his elbow. "It's big," I said.

"It's more stable for a *young man* if it goes onto the upper arm." Dr. Adams looked at the nurse. "You can take out the IV now, nurse." Then he handed Billy some papers—he was closer. I was still standing on the other side of Billy. "These are the instructions on how to care for the cast. You know—what to do, what not to do. You can give him acetaminophen if he's in pain, but there shouldn't be much. And keep the arm elevated to reduce swelling. If you have any questions, or something doesn't seem right, don't hesitate to come in." He looked at Aiden. "Hey, big fella. How you feeling?"

Aiden took a deep breath. "Fine." He looked at his arm. "It's blue! You gave me a blue cast!"

"I said I would, didn't I?"

"Yeah, but I thought you were kidding! I have a blue cast, Mommy!"

I was still shaky on my feet, so Billy helped me over to Aiden's side. "It looks very good on you, too, Aiden." What a clichéd thing to say, but I wasn't myself yet.

The doctor turned around, opened a drawer, and returned with something in his hand.

Aiden shied as if he was afraid the doctor was going to do something bad to him. Although I hated to see that, what could I do? But the doctor smiled and said, "Relax,

Aiden. I did such a good job on your cast that I'm going to sign my work! Hold still." He braced the cast with one hand and with the other he signed his name with a black felt marker. "There! How's that?"

"That's cool!" Aiden smiled at the signature on his cast.

The doctor turned toward me. "He'll need to have the cast removed in six weeks."

Aiden was almost wide awake now, and he was disturbed. "Oh, no! How soon can I go back to karate?"

The doctor looked at Billy for confirmation. When Billy nodded, the doctor said. "Now, I thought you were kidding, Aiden! I'm afraid you won't be doing any karate until the cast comes off."

Aiden made a swipe with his right arm, as if he was hitting a piece of wood. "Not even with just my good arm?"

"'Fraid not," said the doctor. "All right. Bye now. You'll be fine, Aiden." And he trooped through the curtained doorway without even pushing the curtain aside.

CHAPTER FORTY-ONE

I DIDN'T WANT Aiden to think about how much he would miss karate, so I picked up the black marker the doctor had placed on the counter. "Here, Aiden. Let me and Billy sign your cast now, too."

Aiden's downtrodden expression immediately changed to a smile, and he moved the cast away from his body to give me easier access. I signed the cast with a flourish and handed the marker to Billy. After Billy finished, we stepped away to admire our work. Aiden did, too. Then we wondered if we were free to leave or if we had to stay to be officially released.

When the nurse removed Aiden's IV, she had left the room and taken the IV contraption with her. And while I was wondering what to do, she returned holding a blue sling for Aiden. "Here you go, Aiden. This will help you." After she helped him sit up, she slipped the sling over his head and showed him how it worked. "It will make you more comfortable. Bye, now, Aiden." She smiled at us, handed me the follow-up instructions, and disappeared through the curtain.

Billy leaned over to Aiden, who still sat on the

examining table. "You want me to carry you? Are you still tired from the sedative? Or do you want to walk?"

"I'm a little tired, but I can walk. Maybe it will wake me up a little," Aiden said in a soft little voice that made me feel bad for him.

"Wait! He needs a shirt on. He can't leave with the hospital gown on. I can't believe that the nurse didn't notice that."

"It's because they're so busy out there. I bet all these rooms are filled now." He turned toward Aiden. "Good thing Mommy is here, huh, Aiden? We would have walked you out of here with your hospital gown on!"

Aiden shrugged his shoulders. "I don't care," he said, still sounding sleepy.

"Well, let's take off the gown first." Billy helped him pull the gown over his cast. "And now what about your sweatshirt? It won't fit over that cast." He looked at me. "Should we cut the sleeve off?"

"No!" said Aiden. "It's my favorite sweatshirt! Can't you put it on me without that arm?" It made me feel a special kind of warmth that his favorite sweatshirt was from the place where I worked.

"Sure we can. Here. Just put it over his head and put his good arm in. Like this." I stepped over to Aiden. "Raise your right arm, Aiden." He did, and I pulled the sweatshirt over his head with his right arm in the sleeve. The other sleeve just hung there at his side and gave me a sick feeling.

Then Billy lifted him off the table and put him on the floor. Aiden grabbed my hand, and we walked out. As soon as we got to a clear area, Billy put his arm around Aiden as we walked.

When we got to the truck, Billy put Aiden inside and

fastened his seat belt. I got in the other side and sat next to him. Billy stepped into the driver's seat and started the engine.

"Where's Bingo?" asked Aiden, panicky.

"He's right here with me, Aiden," said Billy, as Bingo stood up on his hind legs and looked over the seat at Aiden.

"Oh, okay, good," said Aiden.

Halfway home, Billy pulled into a drive-thru that we all agreed on. Billy and I got a burger and fries, and Aiden got a fish sandwich. I didn't even know he liked fish. Maybe it was a change of taste from having the broken arm. After Billy parked the truck, we ate silently without going inside. I'm not sure if any of us—except maybe Billy—had the energy to get up and walk.

We finished eating and resumed the trip home. Five minutes later, Aiden's head was leaning on my shoulder, and I could tell by his breathing that he was asleep.

"Aiden's sleeping. Thank you for rushing over and taking us to the hospital and taking care of us and all."

Billy smiled into the rearview mirror. "It's my pleasure, ma'am."

"You know Billy, I've been thinking and—"

"Uh oh," said Billy without letting me finish. Then he chuckled.

"Come on, listen. You know the anonymous phone call about John, and it turned out to be close but a lie?"

"Yes."

"It seems strange to me that Derek was outside when the phone call came in, but entered the building just in time to pick it up from dispatch. You know, almost like he knew it was coming in. It makes me think he made the phone call himself."

"That's a big leap, Lorry."

"It bothers me about the thing with Zack, too. They're not friends. I asked Zack. He told me this in confidence, so don't say anything to Derek, but just listen. Derek picked him up, drove him around, and asked him about his alibi, which was solid. I almost had the feeling that Derek would have made another anonymous phone call if Zack wasn't covered. And the thing with Nick stealing his sunglasses. It's too much, Billy. He's hiding something, and I think what he's hiding is that his sister killed her husband."

"That makes a certain amount of sense. He has been acting erratically, but I attributed it to stress from me having to let one of the deputies go. I *have* been thinking of revisiting the wife. When I think about it, maybe she was either holding back or hiding something. And I need to find out what that was. Maybe it was her, or she might be able to lead me to someone who had something against her husband. Someone she's protecting. The investigation is going no where right now, and it needs to move forward."

Aiden moaned in his sleep and moved himself closer against me. His cast pushed against my side and was uncomfortable, but I didn't want to disturb him by moving away. He needed me right now, and I wouldn't let a little discomfort stop that.

"Is he okay?" Billy asked.

"Yeah, he's fine."

"We're almost home."

I looked up, and we were just crossing the bridge from Coyote Moon to Rutledge. In another minute we were home. Billy stepped out of the truck to walk around to Aiden's side. Aiden woke up when Billy's door closed, and for a second he didn't know where he was. Then he looked down at the cast on his arm.

"Oh. It wasn't a dream then."

"No, sweetie, you really broke your arm." I unhooked his seat belt for him.

Billy opened the door, scooped Aiden out, carried him across the yard, and while holding him up with one of his strong arms, he deftly unlocked the front door and carried him into the house, with me and Bingo following behind. Billy took Aiden into his room, with Aiden complaining the whole while that he wasn't tired. "Let's just put your jammies on. You don't have to go to sleep yet. How's that?"

"All right," said Aiden without much fight in him.

I stood in the doorway while Billy helped Aiden take his pants off and put on the bottoms of his pajamas. Then Billy gently eased the sweatshirt off him. But when he got to putting the top of his pajamas on, there was the same problem. He looked at me.

"You're the clothes hound, Lorry. What can we do about this? Unless you don't care if we cut off the sleeve, Aiden."

"No! I like these pajamas! I don't want to ruin them."

"How about if you wear one of my nightgowns for your top?" I asked.

"But you're a girl. I don't want to wear a girl-thing."

"Oh, Aiden," I sighed.

"No, no. I get this," said Billy. "I understand completely. How 'bout this, Aiden?" Billy unbuttoned his sheriff's uniform shirt, took it off, and held it up for Aiden. "I'm pretty sure my sleeves are big enough that your cast will fit right through."

Aiden's tired eyes lit up. "Really, Sheriff Billy? You'd

let me wear your shirt to bed?"

"Sure thing!" said Billy, as he eased the cast into the left sleeve and then slid Aiden's right arm into the other sleeve. "Fits perfect!"

Aiden looked down at the shirt that still had Billy's sheriff's badge on it, and he raised his eyes. Billy, always thinking, said, "Gotta take this off so it doesn't poke you while you sleep." He undid the badge and slipped it into his front pants pocket.

Aiden smiled. "I figured you couldn't leave it there. But just wearing your shirt is great! Thanks so much, Sheriff Billy!"

"Now, should we read your book?"

Aiden yawned. "You know, I am pretty tired after all. I think I just want to go to sleep." He put his head on the pillow and then sat back up. "Oh! I forgot to tell you something important! There is an assembly the night before Thanksgiving, and I will be reciting a couple of poems!"

"Aiden that's great!" I said.

Aiden looked down at his cast. "Do you think I can still do it with this on?"

"Oh, Aiden," said Billy, "I think you could do it with both hands tied behind you and one foot in a sling!"

The smile returned to Aiden's face. "Thanks, Sheriff Billy!"

Billy kissed him on the forehead and walked to the door. As I walked toward Aiden's bed, I passed him and he squeezed my hand. Then I kissed Aiden on the forehead and made sure he was tucked in good with the cast outside the covers. "I think you'll be more comfortable this way. G'night, son. I love you."

"I love you, too, Mommy." Aiden turned over, and I

would have bet that he was asleep in minutes.

Billy waited for me in the hall, and we walked out to the living room together. We sat on the couch and Billy, bare chested, put his arm around me.

"Thanks again for rescuing us today." He made a motion with his hand which I took to mean *think nothing of it*. "I feel so bad about causing him to break his arm. I'll never be able to forgive myself for that. I'm such a bad mother." Tears would have come to my eyes, but I didn't think I deserved even that small luxury.

Billy pulled away and looked at me. "You are not! How'd you cause it? I thought he fell off a ladder."

"He did, but it was because he thought I didn't want to do the high part of the exhibit." I sniffled, feeling sorry for myself that I was such a piece of garbage mother that I would break my own kid's arm.

Putting his arm back around me, he grabbed my shoulder and shook it gently. "Lorry. You did not cause that kid to climb up that ladder and fall off. He used bad judgment. And I know that you and I both—I'm as guilty as you—sometimes think of Aiden as an adult because he is so mature. But he is a kid. He's seven years old. And seven-year-olds sometimes make bad decisions. Did you tell him you didn't want to do the exhibit?"

"No, I didn't tell him that."

"Why didn't you do it?"

"Because I was working all morning on some stuff that Martha gave me. I would have done it if it hadn't been for that. I ran out of time."

"So even that wasn't your fault."

"But I really didn't want to do it."

"It doesn't matter, Lorry. Even if you didn't, it doesn't matter. Would you have ever given him permission to go up that ladder?"

I shook my head vehemently. "Never," I replied.

"Lorry, you need to let this go. It was not your fault. Kids get hurt sometimes. This was not in any way your fault."

Turning my body, I snuggled into his and buried my face in his neck. "Thank you for saying that, Billy. I appreciate it." I felt so grateful that he had told me that —even though I still wasn't sure it was true.

CHAPTER FORTY-TWO

AS I SAT in my car behind the Rutledge Historical Society, I thought over the events of the weekend and the morning. Saturday morning had been depressing with Aiden refusing to either get out of his pajamas or leave his room. Part of that was because he didn't want to take off Billy's shirt. But the rest of it was his general unhappiness over his broken arm and how it would limit his activities. Even when Billy came over, he wouldn't come out.

That all changed when Mason and Petra popped over unexpectedly at noon bearing pizza. And it was Aiden's favorite pizza—double pepperoni. He would settle for *just* pepperoni, but he preferred double pepperoni. And unfortunately, as much as I liked pepperoni, double pepperoni always gave me indigestion. Oh, well, you can't look a gift pizza in the pepperoni, if you know what I mean.

Mason and Petra both signed Aiden's cast, which made him feel a little better. During lunch, Aiden had told the sad tale of not being able to practice karate until the cast was off and how sad that made him. Mason, looking for any opportunity he could get and much to my dismay, suggested to Aiden that he would teach him how to play chess. They played most of Saturday afternoon, and of course, Aiden picked it right up.

I had played chess when I was a kid and had been dragged to this tournament and that tournament all over. Of course, it wasn't my mother who had done the dragging, I was escorted back and forth by one of *the help*. I can't even say who, since they changed so often. I had barely gotten one's name down when that person left and another appeared. It wasn't easy working for my mother. She was a tyrant. That went on for years. You don't become a chess master at eighteen years old without a lot of practice.

Anyway, when it came to teaching Aiden to play chess, I didn't want him to go through all that—the being dragged to each tournament part, not the help part. It made perfect sense to me. My mother forced me to go, so I was not even going to teach Aiden to play. That would solve that.

Petra, sixteen-year-old Petra, showed me the error of my ways. She said I was being just as bad as my mother, because what if Aiden *wanted* to play chess? Then I was keeping him from it, which was as bad as my mother forcing me to go. Okay, okay. I know she's sixteen, but you have to accept wisdom from wherever it might come.

At four o'clock, Martha and Hugo stopped over with a casserole. An hour later after we all visited and everyone had signed Aiden's cast, everybody piled into the kitchen to eat. Billy had to put the extra leaf in the table. After dinner, we talked some more, and then everyone left, leaving just the three of us, Billy, me, and Aiden. Was Aiden ever tired! It had been another long day for him, but he was happier now and not feeling sorry for himself any more.

Sunday, Billy and I took turns playing chess with Aiden, and by the end of the day, Aiden had beaten Billy two times. It would be a while before he could beat me! He still had a thing or two to learn. But he was proud of himself and feeling good, and that's all that mattered.

Monday, I gave Aiden the choice: come with me to work or go to school. And he very eagerly chose school. But we went early so I could talk to Pamela Reilly about Aiden's arm. She made a fuss over his cast, signed it, and sent him in to sit with Marylou in the outer office while she and I talked. And then she asked, "How do you feel?"

"What do you mean?"

"I mean, are you blaming yourself for this?"

"Yes," I said, not expecting the question.

Pamela nodded. "Most parents do. Unless you pushed him off that ladder, Lorry, you are not at fault. I know Aiden is almost more like an adult than a kid, but he is seven, Lorry! He's a kid! Kids sometimes have bad judgment. This is not your fault. Neither is it his—he's a kid. Let it go and stop blaming yourself!"

"Okay," I said sheepishly.

I don't think she believed that I would let it go, so she said, "That's an order!" in a stern voice.

That made me laugh, and so I saluted her and said, "Yes, captain!"

Then I had left the school, but I left with a smile instead of a self-pitying frown, and there I was parked behind the historical society. It was still early, but it was time to go in.

CHAPTER FORTY-THREE

BINGO AND I walked in the back door and made our way to the front. As we walked down the hall, Petra called out, "Lorry, how's Aiden doing?"

We reached her desk and as Bingo jumped on her, she put her face down so he could kiss her. "He's doing much better since Mason taught him to play chess. He's gotten reasonably competent just playing over the weekend."

"See?" She didn't say the whole thing, "I told you so." But I knew that was her intent.

"Yes, Petra." I bent my head and put my hands together in front of my chest. "You are the wise one."

That made us both laugh. She reached down, unhooked Bingo's leash, and handed it to me. "Listen, Lorry, I wanted to tell you that I'll be in late tomorrow. I wanted to make sure you'd be here to open."

"Sure, I'll be here. No problemo. What's goin' on?"

"I have to meet with my counselor for the online school stuff."

"Nothing wrong is it? You're doing your studying okay?" Suddenly I felt a huge wave of guilt rush over me, making me feel like I was having a hot flash, which, let me tell you, I'm much too young for. But I had been asking her to fill in for me so much lately, I worried that she hadn't been doing her work.

"Oh, no, nothing like that. I just have to check in periodically, and they ask questions about how I'm doing mentally, am I pushing myself too hard, not hard enough, do I still like the program—you know, stuff like that. It's all pretty routine."

"Oh, thank goodness," I said.

"Whaat?"

"Nothing. That's good, that's all I meant. That's good."

"Anyway, I've got to get back to it now."

"It's still early. I'm going next door to get breakfast. Helping Aiden get dressed took longer than I expected, and I didn't get to eat. But I'll leave the *Closed* sign up so no one bothers you."

"'k." She had already turned back to her computer, and I wasn't even sure she was listening.

Bingo followed me to the door, but I pointed toward the back and said, "Bingo, go to Rocky." He didn't have to be asked twice. He loved that cat.

Unlocking the front door, I left the *Closed* sign up and walked next door to the cafe. I walked in, saw Kasey, and smiled at her. She nodded without expression. While waiting for her at the counter, I looked around the room. Most of the tables were filled. Kasey picked up some dishes at an empty table, walked past me, put them in a container in the back of the counter, and looked at me.

"Oh," I said, half expecting her to say *something*, anything, "I just want to get another egg mcmuffin and a large coffee."

"Lorry!" she said, softly but with a distinct edge to it.

"Why do you do this to me? I already told you that we don't carry that!"

"Oh, that's right," I said. "Sorry, I meant one of those egg sandwiches with ham on an English muffin. I thought you knew what I meant."

Kasey scribbled down my order so hard that it must have torn through to the paper beneath. "Lorry," she whispered with rage seething just below the surface, "I know how you feel about me. I know you used to call me Cruella Deville, just because I took your boyfriend in first grade!"

"You knew about that?" I asked, grimacing. Color me embarrassed. I liked calling her that; it made people laugh. But I never knew that she knew about it, and worse, that it had come from me.

"Of course I knew about it. Kids talked about it not exactly behind my back. And you probably still call me that! He wasn't even that cute!"

"I don't call you that anymore, Kasey." That was true, but it was only a month or two since I had stopped. But Conrad Hayes *was* cute. Black hair and sky blue eyes.

"So you say!" She turned around and fastened my order on the rack between her and the kitchen. The cook grabbed it right off. Good, I was hungry.

"Look, I'm sorry, Kasey. I was wrong, and I apologize. But I'd like to ask you something about Chuck."

"Chuck?" she asked, like she didn't know who I was talking about. Wow, we forget so quickly. "Oh, yeah. What?"

"You know, Charles. Do you know if he had any enemies? Anyone who had something against him?"

She looked up casually and moved her eyes to her left. "Shhh. That's his wife." And then as I got ready to turn my head and look, she whispered, "No, don't turn around. Look later. She's wearing the blue and red blouse." I nodded, and she continued, so low that I could barely hear her. "No, I don't know of any enemies or anyone who had anything against him. She"—Kasey indicated the wife—"probably knew about us and therefore had something against him. But I don't know who else might. He was a likable guy."

My order came then, and she wrapped it up, poured and put a lid on the coffee, and put it into a paper bag. She rang it up on the register and put her hand out for the money. "Anything else?" she said under her breath.

"That's all I can think of for now. If you think of anything—anything at all that you think might help—just let me know. You know where I am," I said smiling, trying to lighten the mood. "Or wait till tomorrow. Petra will be in late, so I'll be in early. I'll probably need breakfast and coffee again, so I'll see ya then."

Kasey nodded and said, "I heard Aiden broke his arm. He okay?"

I did think it was funny that she never called over the weekend. I was sure that someone would have mentioned Billy carrying him into the truck the other day. "Yeah, he got a cast on and now he's learning to play chess since he can't do karate for six weeks."

"Ah, like Momma like son, huh?"

"Well, he's already gotten really good just over the weekend," I said, shrugging. "Hey, how's Lily doing?"

Kasey looked at me defiantly. "Lily and I are both doing fine, thank you."

I took a step backwards and looked at my watch. "Anyway, I gotta get back. Talk to you later, Kasey."

"Yeah," she said without a smile.

As I turned away from her, I saw Chuck's wife. She wore a gaudy blue and red blouse. Although I couldn't see her pants, I would bet on it that they didn't match. Her face was plain with too much makeup, her hair cut short and in tiny curls—like someone had left the permanent solution on too long—and she had a rude look on her face. It wasn't like she was sad and grieving her husband, it was like she was ticked off at the world. And she was much older than Kasey, or at least looked much older. No wonder Chuck Jones wanted to mess around with other women. Oh! There I was being judgmental again. It's hard to break a habit, you know?

CHAPTER FORTY-FOUR

BACK AT MY desk, I unwrapped the breakfast sandwich, took a sip of coffee and a bite of sandwich, and thought about the last ten minutes. Kasey was angry at me, and, if I thought about it, she had every right to be. I *had* called her Cruella Deville years longer than I should have. Maybe she had been stuffing all the anger all these years and only allowed it to come out now because of all the rigamarole over the murder. Or, she had just let it go all these years, and now it came burbling up because of the murder. I would bet on the second. Kasey wasn't the type to stuff anger. Then again, Kasey wasn't who I thought she was.

After I went over every syllable of the conversation with Kasey, I thought again about Chuck's wife and the way she looked. That rude expression. And when the answer came to me, I almost dropped my not-quite-egg-mcmuffin into my lap. She had heard me asking Kasey questions! I had accused Kasey so many times about not keeping her mouth shut, and here I was doing the same thing!

I closed my eyes and tilted my head toward the ceiling.

"Oh no, oh no, oh no," I said to myself. Hoping that I said it quietly enough that it didn't draw Petra's attention, I clapped my hand over my mouth and tried not to utter the moan that was building up inside. Billy was going to kill me. It's one thing to ask Kasey questions when she was here and no one else was around, but how stupid of me to ask her questions in such a public establishment as the Koffee Korner Kafe. How stupid could I get?

Beating my head against the wall wouldn't help, although once Billy heard about it, he might beat my head against the wall for me. And I would deserve it, too. I couldn't even blame him. So, at that moment, I did what any red-blooded American woman would do. I finished my sandwich and coffee and went to the new exhibit to get my mind off what I had done. It couldn't be undone, so what else could I do?

When I looked up at the new exhibit, I smiled. Petra had finished cleaning out the old exhibit and had put up several new pictures on the high part of the exhibit. She had also put away the dreaded ladder. I didn't even notice that when I walked in this morning.

"Thank you, Petra!" I walked to her desk, and she turned around and smiled at me. "An extra thanks is in order, because I know how busy you are. And especially for putting away that ladder. I have half a notion to burn the darn thing!"

"I was happy to do it. Since the upper part of the exhibit was what got Aiden up there to begin with, I figured that I'd get it out of the way so he wasn't tempted again."

Holding my fist out in front of me, I shook it and said, "He better not try that stunt again!"

"Yeah, I bet you'd hit him—about as much as you'd hit me!"

I took a step closer and waved my fist in her face, which she pushed away. "Besides," she continued, "I needed a break. I've been hitting my studies too hard. I'm a little afraid that tomorrow I'll get in trouble for being *too far ahead* of where I'm supposed to be."

"Seriously? You can get in trouble for that?"

She shrugged. "I'll find out tomorrow."

"Well, anyway, thanks Petra. Aiden and I both appreciate your efforts." I walked back to the exhibit and looked at it. There was a sign at the top of the exhibit that said *Who Killed Edward?* One eight by ten of the victim—must be Edward—was accompanied by small portraits of several serious men as well as a class picture with twelve youngsters in it, girls and boys. The portraits of the men were supposedly the suspects in the murder. No women? Women could be killers, too. And just beneath the small portraits, Petra had put up a picture of the attorney and next to that the results of the polygraph test. No wonder it interested Aiden.

Then I started pawing through the box containing the rest of the stuff. Inside the box—however did they get it, I wondered—was the bloodied shirt of the guy who was killed. And the gun was on the bottom of the box. I didn't dare touch it. Aiden knew more about guns than I did. I would have to get Billy to rectify that and teach me a thing or two about guns. Better to be safe than sorry, as they say. When the phone rang, I stood up and ran to the front so Petra wouldn't be tempted to answer.

"Rutledge Historical Society. How can I help you? . . . Yes, we close at five. . . . No, the new exhibit isn't up yet, probably after Thanksgiving. . . . Okay. Bye now."

When I put the phone down, I heard Bingo upstairs growling softly. He and Rocky did this really funny thing. They both got into the yoga downward dog position—I don't do yoga, but I've seen the picture of it enough times—where their front legs are stretched out in front of them and their butts are in the air. Then Bingo growls, Rocky hisses, and they circle each other in that position, and after a few minutes, they stand up, sniff each other's butts, and lay down cuddled up together. It's the cutest thing.

Turning to my computer, I saw that Martha had sent me an email. The subject was "I'm so slow!" and said she needed me to type up a few more documents for her. That made me laugh.

Then I heard heavy male feet approaching from the back, but it didn't sound like Billy. Turning from my desk to see who was coming down the hall, I saw that it was Derek the deputy.

He walked by Petra as if he didn't see her, because he probably didn't. With a grim expression on his face, he said, "Is Billy here?"

"No. Is he supposed to be?"

"I'm just looking for him, that's all." He turned around to stomp back off down the hall.

I tried to think pleasant thoughts about him because Billy had said to give the poor guy a chance. He *had* lost his brother-in-law, and maybe they were close. So I decided to give him a chance, and I stood up and followed him for several paces.

"Hey, Derek? I was wondering if you could help me with something? There's a big box in my car. Any chance you can bring it in for me? I'd appreciate it if you could."

"I don't have time for that! I have law work to do!" He continued stomping down the hall, and I heard the back door slam behind him. So much for giving him a chance.

CHAPTER FORTY-FIVE

WALKING BACK PAST Petra, I saw Rocky sitting on the edge of her desk grooming himself. Sitting back down at my desk, I checked for any other emails besides Martha's, and then the front door opened to the accompaniment of the jingling bell. It was Martha's messenger boy. He handed me the manila envelope, and I smiled at him. He smiled back shyly. Sitting back down at my desk, I began the first step which was editing the documents. Then I began to type.

When I finished typing the first one, a thought occurred to me and my blood ran cold. Had I left that pistol from the old murder case out? Maybe it was illegal that we even had it. What did I know about stuff like that? So I raced to the back and found it safely tucked away under a bunch of stuff—including the blood-stained shirt—inside the box. Returning to the front, I kept typing.

The last document still needed editing, so I had to do that before I typed it. I finished typing, sent everything off to Martha, had time to use the restroom, and Aiden walked in the door with a huge smile on his face.

"Look at my cast, Mommy! *Every*body wanted to sign it! Doesn't it look cool?"

After carefully looking at the cast and remarking how cool it was, I opened my arms and Aiden fell into them, pressing the hard cast against my back. Hugging Aiden was worth it. We separated, and he looked and saw that the top of the exhibit was finished.

"Mommy! You did it! *Thank* you."

I glanced down the hall, and Petra was sticking her head out where I could just see her. Aiden couldn't. She motioned with her hand and nodded her head that I took to mean she would allow me to get the credit for it. But I couldn't do it. Not lie to my own son. No, that was just wrong.

Kneeling down, I put my hands on his shoulders. "Aiden, I was going to, but Petra got there before me. She is the one who did this." With this confession, I could barely look into his eyes.

But he smiled and said, "Well, she did a great job." He raised his voice, so she would be sure to hear and said, "Thanks, Petra! Great job!"

Aiden and I worked on the exhibit for the rest of the day, dragging stuff out of the box, evaluating it, putting it into the exhibit or saving it for discussion later. When it came to the bloody shirt, we had a civilized but intense discussion.

"It's important for this piece to be in the exhibit. It's crucial evidence!"

Now he sounded just like Billy. "It's too gruesome for most people. I think we should leave it out."

"That boy with the dress on in that exhibit is too gruesome for most people," he replied. He was talking about the clothing exhibit from the 1800s. It showed a little boy with a skirt and blouse on. All the little boys were horrified at it—and apparently that included Aiden.

"It's not the same, Aiden. This is a real person's blood. You can't glorify that." Sometimes I worried that I talked over his head, but he had a better vocabulary than I did. It was his constant reading that did it.

"It's not glorifying his death. I want to put it up there to *solve* his murder."

"Aiden, this happened more than fifty years ago. How is anyone here going to solve his murder now? That's silly."

He put his hand on his hip and sighed. "Mom"—he pronounced it in two syllables—"it's called a cold case, and you never know. Maybe some new information will come forth."

That conversation went on for ten unfruitful minutes, and I finally relented and agreed to bring in a hanger the next day to display the bloody thing. That was because Aiden thought if it was hung up nicely on a hanger, then it would display its importance in the exhibit. And this was a seven-year-old. Would I even be able to talk to him when he was ten?

The gun would naturally go in the exhibit, locked of course, and there were other objects and other pictures he wanted to put there, too. He left the gun in the bottom of the box with other stuff on top of it, and we walked back to my desk to get my purse before leaving.

"Petra, I'll see you tomorrow—whenever you get in. Not to worry, I will be here on time to open."

"I wasn't worried, Lorry. I knew you would be." She looked at Aiden and held out her arms to him. "Come here, you. How'd it go at school today with your new cast. It looks like everybody signed it, huh?"

He hugged her and nodded. "Everybody! There's almost no room left, so I'm glad you and Mason were my first friends to sign it."

The phone rang, and I looked at my watch. It was five o'clock on the nose. I thought I'd better get it. Besides, I hadn't heard from Billy all day, and I was hoping it was him. It was. He was still in Coyote Moon as he had been all day, and he wanted to know about dinner. I told him there was enough pizza and casserole for him and Aiden, and I would fix something for myself. And Billy, dear one that he is, said he'd pick up something special for me. What a guy. Between having Billy as a boyfriend and Aiden as a son, I didn't think I could get much luckier.

CHAPTER FORTY-SIX

AIDEN AND I got home, and he had to show me all the names on his cast along with a short biography of each person. He was so cute when he was doing it, and he made the stories so appealing that it was very entertaining. Even Bingo sat there listening to him, wagging his tail and looking fascinated.

Not long after Aiden finished his stories, Billy came in. Aiden ran up to him and threw himself in Billy's strong arms. "Sheriff Billy!"

"How ya doin', little pard? That cast treating you okay?"

"Yeah! It's fine! Look at all the signatures I got!"

"That's awesome, Aiden. Let me say hello to your Mommy now." Billy put Aiden down and held out his arms to me. I fell into them.

"Hello, Sheriff Billy," I said. "Good to see you."

He kissed me and handed me the paper bag in his hand. It smelled good. I opened the bag, and it was a Coyote Moon Casino buffalo burger, my favorite. After I gave him another hug, I went into the kitchen to heat the pizza and casserole for the two of them, and the buffalo burger for me. And while I did that, Aiden gave Billy a rundown on the signatures on his cast.

We ate and talked and watched a short movie, and when Aiden went to bed—after Billy helped him put his pajamas on and then read to him—we sat on the couch together. I usually talked to Billy once or twice during the day, so I was really missing him. Plus, we had business to discuss. *His* business, of course, but even so.

"So, did you see Chuck's wife?" I asked.

"Chuck?" Billy said, narrowing his eyes at me. "Don't tell me you *knew* him, too."

"Billy, come on! I want to know!"

He laughed. "Yes, that's why I was in Coyote Moon. I wanted to talk to her while she was at work. I figured she might be more forthcoming that way."

"And was she?"

"Yes, she was. She confessed Derek had told her to tell me that she didn't already know about the affair. When I looked concerned, she begged me not to come down on him because he was just trying to protect her. And then she apologized for lying to me before."

"Anything else?"

Billy nodded. "Yeah. She said she not only knew about Kasey and Amanda Fletcher, but there were plenty of others, and she knew about them, too."

"What's her name, by the way?"

"Her name is Jane. Jane Jones."

"Jane Jones? Oh, no! If I were her, I would have kept my maiden name!" There I was being judgmental again, but I'm telling you, sometimes the words pop out before I have time to stifle them.

Billy pulled away and looked at me. "Ah, so you don't like Jones. What do you think of Madrigal?"

216

His comment took me so much by surprise that I had nothing to say. Imagine. Me with nothing to say. Madrigal was Billy's last name. That was the second time in a week that he said anything like that to me, and I still had no idea how I should respond. But Billy's unwavering eyes were still on me, so I had to either say something clever or blurt out the wrong thing—one of the two. "I, uh, um—"

Billy, without changing his expression or even a slight smile, moved back up against me and said, "Yes, as I was saying, at that point, *Mrs. Jones*, looked down and said under her breath, 'I married him for his money. So I didn't care what he did or who he slept with.' Then she looked back up at me with a defiant expression and said, 'And I have my own boyfriend, as well.'"

"Wow, wow, wow. I'm not sure what to make of that."

"Well, it takes jealousy out as far as motive goes."

"She could still be lying, though, right?"

"I don't think so. I asked for his name, and she said she wanted to talk to him before giving it out—because he was married, too."

"Honor among thieves, huh?"

Billy nodded. "Something like that." He leaned against me and pressed his lips to my cheek. "Anyway, that's about it. Oh, no, there was one other thing I almost forgot. When she had given work as her alibi the first time I talked to her, I called and verified with her boss. This time I went in to the boss to verify the time. The boss said she had arrived early that day, so she was definitely there. When I asked if she often arrived early, the boss said, no, never. And not only that, but she only worked part-time, so coming in early and staying late wasn't expected.

217

"So when I was in the interview with Mrs. Jones, I asked her why she came in early that day when she had never come in early before. She said because she hadn't gotten all her work done the day before."

"I don't understand what you're getting at."

"Mrs. Jones had worked there for three years, and she had never come in to work early before, and it wasn't expected of her. Certainly in that three years there must have been some other time when she didn't get all her work done. So why did she come in early that day and never before? Had she suddenly become more conscientious, or was it something else? That bothers me."

CHAPTER FORTY-SEVEN

THE FOLLOWING MORNING it took forever to get Aiden dressed again. He didn't want to cut up any of his sweatshirts and none of them would fit over his cast. Aiden wanted to wear a t-shirt, but it was too cold for that. Finally, since we would be late if the *discussion* continued, I allowed him to wear the sweatshirt he had worn the day before. I actually allowed him to take it out of the dirty clothes basket to wear it. Horrors. It was a little big for him, and the cast fit through perfectly. Sometime today, I'd have to go to the thrift store and pick up some shirts and a jacket that would fit him.

So when I dropped him off for school and drove back to the society and parked, I had that on my mind. And that must be why I *accidentally* left Bingo in the car when I walked in through the back door like I do every other day.

When I closed the door behind me, I heard a shuffling and then a shadow came out from the curtained closet. I didn't even have time to consider if it was Billy again, because the man grabbed me so hard and held me so tight, not to mention that he had his hand pressed so hard against my mouth that my teeth cut me on the inside. I could taste the blood.

"Listen," he said in a hoarse whispered voice. "*Stay* out of this. It is no concern of *yours*. If you continue sticking your big, fat nose where it doesn't belong, you and *your family* will be in trouble. *Big* trouble. I'll *get* you! Now stay out of it!" Then he gave me a hard shove, sending me sprawling onto the cement floor where I scraped both knees and shredded my pantyhose. I heard the back door slam behind him, not even giving me a chance to turn around and look at who it was.

There was no way I could get up right away. The fright of the experience had my heart racing, and I was shocked to discover that tears flowed out of my eyes. When the pain from my scraped knees started throbbing, I knew I had to get up. First, I got up on my hands and knees, which hurt my knees more than ever. That's what I get for wearing such short skirts at my age. No, actually, when he pushed me, the skirt flew up above my knees. Just as well. I like this skirt. It's my blue print that I wear with a solid blue blouse. The jerk didn't even compliment me before he gave me that shove.

When I struggled to my feet, I hoped that I hadn't gotten any blood on my skirt, but alas, I did. It could have been worse. I might have broken something when I landed. But the only thing broken was my pride. I should've kicked him! I should've screamed! I should've bitten his hand! But the truth was that it happened so suddenly, I didn't have time to even think about doing any of those things. And he had his hand too tight on my mouth for me to even open it. Taking a deep breath, I tried to calm myself. Finally, when my heart got to some semblance of normal, I took a few steps to see if I could walk without falling down on my face again.

My knees still throbbed, but otherwise I was okay. I made it into the bathroom and looked in the mirror. My nose wasn't big and fat! How dare he say that! You're wondering why the first thing I did was look in the mirror after that experience? I'm vain, that's why. And if someone calls my nose big and fat, I have to look. So sue me. That's just the way I am. Next, I pulled some paper towels from the rack, and after pulling off the ruined pantyhose, washed both knees and then put bandages on them. Then I rinsed the skirt as best as I could. When I finished, I wanted to go get Bingo from the car, but I didn't have the nerve to go out that back door.

So I did the only sensible thing I could think of. Through throbbing knees and all, I struggled up the stairs and sat on the chair up there. Then I called Rocky, who jumped down from his perch on the high shelf—where he likes to hide—and jumped into my lap. I began stroking him, and he began purring. There is nothing quite as good for the soul as a purring cat on your lap. He wasn't Bingo, and he'd never give me the solace that Bingo gave me on an everyday basis, but I did appreciate Rocky for who he was. And right now he was the one who calmed my nerves and made me feel somewhat normal.

When my stomach growled, I remembered that I hadn't eaten yet. I had to call Billy. I knew that. And yet I was afraid of what he would say. Had I left the back door unlocked? No, never. Of that I was positive. So how did the guy get in? My stomach growled again, and I picked Rocky up and put him on the floor after thanking him for his help. Then I sneezed and rubbed my itching eyes. My cat allergy was better but not gone completely.

Although I needed food, I knew I couldn't face going next door with all those people in there. So I called. My voice broke when Kasey answered the phone, so when I asked if she could bring the food over, she didn't hesitate. She said yes. And I noticed that she had started sounding like the old Kasey again. Next I called Billy, but he was on another line. Then I unlocked the front door and turned the sign to *Open*.

CHAPTER FORTY-EIGHT

SINCE I WAS still too afraid to go out the back door to get Bingo, I turned on the computer, checked my email, and started surfing to sites I thought would make me laugh. None did. I was still too shaken up. When I heard the door jingle behind me, I turned around to see Kasey walk in with a large cup of coffee in one hand and a paper bag in the other. I don't know what came over me in that minute, but the second I saw her, I stood up, wrapped my arms around her, and started weeping on her canary yellow waitress uniform.

She reached behind me and put the coffee and the bag on my desk. "Lorry, what's happened? Are you okay?"

"I am now," I said without releasing her. Then I blubbered out details of what had happened. When I finished, I pulled away from her to show her my knees. My right knee must have been scraped worse than the left, because blood had seeped through the bandage.

"Oh, Lorry!" Kasey grimaced. "That's awful."

"I hate to ask this, Kasey, considering the state of things between us right now. But, you know, did you *tell* anyone I would be alone here this morning?"

Unexpectedly, Kasey doubled over and started laughing. Then she pointed at me. "Lorry, *you* told everyone in the cafe yesterday you would be alone! *Everyone!*"

"Oh, yes," I said and sank into my chair after remembering my revelation of the day before. "You're right. I did that, didn't I?"

"You certainly did!" she said with her hands on her hips. She turned to go and then turned back around. "Oh, I forgot. You wanted to know if Jonesy had any enemies. His wife's—"

"Wait. What? Who's Jonesy?"

"You know, Charles, Chuck, whatever you call him. I called him Jonesy." She smiled in fond remembrance. "He liked that. Anyway, his wife's brother couldn't stand him."

"You mean Derek? The deputy?"

She nodded. "Yeah, that's him. Apparently he begged his sister not to marry him, and then when he found out that Jonesy and I were together, he went ballistic."

While she was talking, I searched my top desk drawer for the note I had found at the post office. I pulled it out, still crumpled, and uncrumpled it. "Kasey, did you write this?"

Kasey took the note and read it, shaking her head. "No, I didn't write it. Where'd you get it?"

"At the post office. In the trash."

"Who wrote it then?" she asked.

Raising my eyebrows, I said, "My guess would be the killer. He or she got Charles-Chuck-Jonesy to come in to the post office early thinking he was meeting you."

"That does make sense," Kasey said.

"Do you recognize the writing at all?"

"No. Not at all. Listen, Lorry, I gotta go."

"Wait! Let me pay you!" I opened the bottom drawer where I keep my purse, and it wasn't there. "Oh, sorry! I left it in the car with Bingo! I'll pay you later."

"Forget it, Lorry. It's on the house." The bell jingled again, and she was out the door.

She said it with a little resentment, but I didn't take it seriously because I knew she was sensitive over me paying her bail. I called Billy's number again and got him.

"Billy? . . . I need you to come over here right away. It's something really important. . . . Yeah, I'll tell you when you get here. . . . And can you get Bingo out of the car for me, please? . . . Why? I'll tell you when you bring him in. . . . Thanks. Love you. Bye."

A couple of minutes later, I heard Bingo's little feet running up the hallway, and then he jumped right into my lap, his tail wagging so hard, I thought it might fall off. He felt cold. I hadn't realized it was that cold in the car.

When I heard Billy's footsteps, before he was even in view, I said, "Billy, is my nose big and fat?"

When he appeared, his hands were on his hips and one of them held my purse, and he looked angry. As big as he was and standing there in front of me like that scared me. Billy had never scared me before, even when he almost held a gun on me. And when he jumped out at me from the closet—although I didn't know that was him. But so fresh from what that guy did, I felt scared. I cowered with my face in Bingo's fur.

"Lorry, is that what you called me here for? Is that what was so important? To look at your nose? And do

225

you know Bingo was *not* in your car but running loose in
the alley! I almost hit him! Your car door was wide open.
And here's your purse. You shouldn't leave it in the car.
What's *wrong* with you today?"

When Bingo jumped into my lap, part of my skirt had
come with him and now one of my knees was showing—
the one that was still bleeding. When Billy noticed that,
he kneeled down and lifted my skirt just enough to see
the entire bandage. "Lorry! What happened? Are you
okay? What is it?"

I lifted my head and all the tears that Bingo's fur had
been absorbing slid down my face. And I found that I
couldn't talk—that's two times in two days—so I put my
face back into Bingo's fur.

Billy leaned over and put his arms around me and
Bingo. Then he stroked my back with his hands, all the
while saying in my ear, "It's okay, Lorry. It will be okay. I
love you. You'll be okay. Tell me what happened. Did
you fall down?"

A few minutes went by with Billy stroking me and
saying sweet things in my ear, and Bingo—already
armed with a heavy winter coat and now Billy pressing
against him with his body heat—starting to pant. In my
face. That dog has the worst breath, and I couldn't take
it much longer, so I picked my head up. The tears hadn't
dried yet, but they weren't flowing like before.

"Billy, something awful happened. Something really
scary."

Bingo jumped down, thankfully, and Billy put his arms
back around me. "Tell me what happened, Lorry. I'm
right here."

And I told him. In excruciating detail, I related the
brief, yet terrifying events of the morning. Billy

continued stroking me for a few minutes after I finished. I have to give him credit for that. Then the investigator in him popped up. There was no keeping it down, of course, I knew that.

He stood up and looked down at me. "Did you leave the back door open?"

"No, I am positive that I didn't."

"Then how would he have gotten in? And how would he know you would be here alone and Petra wouldn't be here?"

Then I unfortunately had to confess how I had shot off my big mouth in the cafe yesterday in front of half the town. And even after my contrite confession, Billy still wasn't happy.

"Oh, Lorry, how could you." It wasn't a question. "You almost got your dog killed, and you could have been killed, too." That must have gotten to him, because he dropped to his knees again and wrapped his arms back around me. I could feel his tears dropping on my back. "I could have lost you. Oh, Lorry, you must be more careful."

Then he sniffed, wiped the tears out of his eyes without saying anything, and stood up. "I'm going to check the back door." When he got there, he called out, "It's locked. But come here, I want to ask you something."

I gathered up what wits I had left about me and walked to the back. He put his hand on the back door and pulled. "You were right. It's locked. But was the deadbolt locked, too?" When I nodded, he turned to the door between the historical society and the cafe next door. He put his hand on the handle and turned. "It's open. Do you check this every night?"

Both doors had deadbolts installed on them since the murder that had taken place several months ago when I first got the job. But I never checked it. "No, Billy, never. Nobody ever uses that door."

Billy frowned, but not at me. "*Some*one did."

I sniffed the air and smelled something perfume-y. Leaning over, I sniffed Billy's face. Nothing.

"What are you doing?"

"Ah, nothing. I just smelled something, that's all."

"If nobody uses this door, I'm going to put a hasp and padlock on it."

"Billy, if I didn't leave the car door open—and I didn't —then that means that the guy who did that to me opened my car door. Can you check it for prints?"

He raised his eyebrows and nodded. Then he keyed his radio attached to his shirt and called for the forensic "team" which consisted of just Derek, since Nick was currently suspended. The idea of Derek coming over to the historical society gave me the heebie-jeebies, though I couldn't tell you why—probably because of the way I saw him treat Zack and Kasey.

Billy leaned over to kiss me. "No more investigating my case! And especially not spreading it all over town! Okay?"

I blinked my eyes coquettishly in response. There was still the note in my desk I wanted to tell him about, but this didn't seem like the right time. He kissed me and walked out the back door.

CHAPTER FORTY-NINE

PETRA CAME IN an hour later, and I told her the whole sorry story. The first thing she said, typical Petra, "Hmmm. Assault. From the Latin, meaning to leap. It's perfect."

"Not now, Petra."

She rubbed my shoulder and gazed at my knee. "At least you weren't badly injured. You could have broken an arm or leg on that cement back there."

I nodded. She was right. It could have been bad. Then again, Aiden and I could have had matching casts. I think he would have liked that. Kind of.

"Listen, Petra, would you mind if I took off for a while? I need to go to the thrift store to get Aiden some temporary clothes to wear that will fit over his cast."

"Can't you cut the arm off on the clothes he already has? Then they would fit perfectly."

"That's what I said. And we argued about it for way too long this morning before I finally let him wear yesterday's shirt. He took it out of the *dirty clothes!*" The thought of it made me groan.

"I bet that actually horrified you, didn't it, Lorry?"

"Are you being smart, Petra? Of course you are, because you are smart. Yes, it horrified me. Anyway, I'm going." I pulled a leash out of my desk and called Bingo as I walked to the back. Then I slipped it on him, and we walked out together. After Billy had come over, it was like he had blessed the place or something, because I wasn't afraid to go out the back door any longer. But I brought a couple of tissues with me so I could wipe the fingerprint dust off my door. That turned out to be hardly necessary, because there wasn't much there. So much for that.

It wasn't until we had driven across the bridge to Coyote Moon that I realized I didn't have my purse with me. So I turned around, drove back across the bridge, down High Street, double parked in the front of the historical society, and ran in to get it. While I was in there, I realized that I had to use the restroom, and when I finished and came outside again, purse on my arm, what do I find on my car? A ticket. I ripped it off the windshield and stuffed it in my purse without even looking at it.

What a jerk that Derek was. Couldn't he even give me a break? No, he probably did it deliberately because I was Billy's girlfriend. And I knew Billy wouldn't cancel it, either. He wasn't that kind of guy. And although that annoyed me, I liked it, too. You know—that he was so honest. Because Eddie was so *not* honest.

The thrift store at the edge of Coyote Moon was a cute little place whose prices were fair. But when I walked around in there looking for size large sweatshirts that might fit Aiden and his accompanying cast, they had nothing. No oversize jackets, either, that might fit him. So I had to go deeper into Coyote Moon to the next thrift store. As I drove there, I wondered if I was being an idiot. After all, I was a multi-millionaire now and could afford to buy him brand new sweatshirts and a new jacket. But it didn't make sense to me to buy sweatshirts that he couldn't wear for years after the cast was removed in six weeks. Maybe Aiden had gotten his frugality from me. So I drove on.

The thrift store I settled on was the Humane Society Thrift Store. They had two of them in Coyote Moon, and this one was smaller, but it was still two or three times as big as the place I had just left. On the window, to the side of the front door, was a sign that said *Welcome to the Coyote Moon Humane Society Thrift Store.* Just beneath that were two numbers that were changed every day. Today, they were five and eight. If one of those numbers matched the last number on your driver's license, then everything you bought that day would be half price. They didn't match. Oh, well. Everybody liked a bargain, including me, and just because I had plenty of money now—which I wasn't at all used to yet—didn't mean that wasn't true.

Walking in the front door, I looked down to my left by the front window and smiled. There were two little bowls of water there for anyone who brought their pets in with them, but I had left Bingo in the car. Still, I had always liked that about this place. The men and boy's department was directly left as you came through the door and then toward the back. Even when I was broke and with Eddy, I bought all my clothes at exclusive stores. It was my only luxury. But when I went out to buy *his* clothes, I bought them here or one of the other thrift stores in town. He didn't care, or maybe it was because he never knew.

The first sweatshirt I saw was perfect for Aiden. It was bright red with a big picture of a horse on the front. Aiden liked horses, and he would love this. Putting the shirt over my arm, I kept perusing the racks. In fifteen minutes, I had found seven shirts that fit the bill and one jacket that would work. It was a little worn, but not bad, and I didn't want to have to drive anywhere else. I wanted to get back to work.

At the cash register, the total came to forty-two dollars. No tax. That was a bargain. I opened my purse, pulled out my wallet, found the hundred I kept in there, and handed it to the cashier. "Can you break that?" I asked. She said yes and handed me the change. They had a big dog piggy bank for donations, and I put all the change in there. I'm cheap, but I can be generous, too—especially where animals are concerned.

CHAPTER FIFTY

WHEN I GOT back to the historical society carting all my treasures inside, I walked right up to Petra and before I even showed her all Aiden's new clothes, I asked her, "I forgot to ask you! I'm sorry. What happened at school today with your counselor?"

"Oh, it was fine. She said it's against the program's policy to allow anyone to graduate high school a year in advance, but she said depending on when I finished, I could maybe enroll in another college class while I was still in high school. That way, I might be able to complete not only my first and second year in college, but possibly a few classes from my third year!"

"Petra, that is so awesome. I'm so proud of you."

She shrugged. "At least someone is."

Petra's parents aren't the most supportive on the planet. Her mother probably would be if it weren't for her fear of Petra's father.

"So what did you get for Aiden? Let me see!"

I brought out the one with the horse, and the blue one with the spaceship, and the black one with Einstein's formula of relativity on it—you know, $E=mc^2$—along with a picture of Einstein. The others weren't so impressive, but I showed her all of them and the raggedy jacket.

"Aiden will love his new clothes! You'll have a lot of washing to do when you get home. You want to go now and get them started?"

"You're so good to me, Petra. No, I'll stay here. I was gone too long already; I only meant to go to the one thrift store on the edge of town, but they had nothing there that would work."

As I walked back to my desk, someone knocked on the door. I put my bags down beside the computer desk and called out "Come on in! It's not locked!" At which point the knocking got louder. "What!" I said.

Then I looked out the window. An old woman stood there, held up by a walker. She had a fierce expression on her heavily lined face, and she was just about to knock on the door with her fist when I opened it.

"Sorry. I didn't realize—"

"Yeah, yeah. You didn't realize I was a cripple. I get it. Are you going to help me in or not?"

"I'm sorry," I said, feeling horrible. I stepped down to boost her up or something—I had no idea what—when she screamed at me again.

"No, no! Just make sure the door doesn't hit me in the face. I can make it up by myself!"

And she did. Then she stood there breathing hard. I hadn't noticed before that she had oxygen coming in through a nasal cannula and a portable tank attached to her walker. But her manner was so tough that I was taken aback, and I stood there not knowing what to say.

"All right," she said after a couple of minutes. "I heard you have a new exhibit up. About a murder. I want to see it."

"I'm sorry, but it's not finished yet. It won't be finished until after Thanksgiving."

"I'm leaving tomorrow for the holidays and won't be back until I don't know when. Maybe not at all if I croak. I want to see it today, and I don't care if it's finished or not."

"Um, okay then. It's back this way." As I walked past Petra's desk, I rolled my eyes. When we got to the exhibit, I let the old woman pass me. "Go ahead and look. Spend as much time as you want."

"Hmmmph," she said as she moved past me.

I looked back after I got back in my office. She was examining the exhibit, and it looked like she was squinting at the pictures on top that Petra had put up. She was in her late eighties and dressed to perfection. I knew expensive clothes when I saw them, and she was wearing very expensive clothes. Her shoes were stable, like an old person might wear, but they, too, were expensive.

The bell on the door jingled and a much younger woman, expensively dressed, stuck her head in. "Did an old woman come in here? With a walker and an oxygen tank?"

Although I hated to give up the old woman—because she seemed to know exactly what she wanted—I couldn't lie to the younger one. So I shrugged and pointed with my thumb behind me. She walked down the hallway.

"Mother! What are you doing here?"

The old woman growled something, but I couldn't hear what she said. And I didn't want to.

"Come on, we're leaving now. Turn around. That's it."

"Don't treat me like I'm senile or helpless! I'm neither!"

"Okay, okay. All right, Mother, I won't."

When they got to my desk, I opened the door for them. As the old woman walked past me, she said, "You're missing two of the suspects up there! One of them is just in the wrong place! Make sure you fix that!"

I nodded and said, "I'll be sure to check that out."

"Be sure you do!" she said as she stepped outside.

The younger woman gave me a *what are you gonna do* look and said, "I'm sorry if she bothered you."

The old woman started shouting something else, but I closed the door so I wouldn't have to get involved in it. I had enough of my own drama going on.

Sitting down at my desk, I remembered the ticket. I dug it out of my purse and walked back in to Petra's office shaking it at her. "Petra! You're not going to believe this! That jerk Derek gave me a ticket for double parking!"

"Well, did you do it?"

"Yes, I did it, but only for a couple of minutes. Besides, that's not the point."

"Lorry, you deserved it," she said and turned back to her computer.

As I walked back to my desk, I looked at the ticket. Something about it looked familiar. I couldn't place it right away no matter how long I stared at it. So I set it aside and checked my email, and then it came to me. Oh, no. Turning back to my desk, I opened the top drawer and pulled out the crumpled note I had showed to Kasey. Then I put the note next to the ticket. The writing matched perfectly.

CHAPTER FIFTY-ONE

THE INFORMATION JUST discovered was too important to be blabbing my mouth off even to Petra. I put the ticket and the note into my purse in the zippered side compartment so I would be sure not to lose either of them. Then I pretended I was having an ordinary day—ordinary if you consider that not only had I been attacked that morning, but I had probably discovered the perpetrator that afternoon—and not to mention, he was undoubtedly the killer, as well.

Aiden came in from school, and I greeted him with a big hug, although he immediately noticed the bandages on my knees. My skirt must have come up just enough for him to see while I hugged him. I consoled him by saying that I had hit the ground hard and skinned both knees. Thankfully, he did not question how I had come to hit the ground, and I did not want to share that information with my seven-year-old son. As protective as he was of me, he'd probably want to start carrying a gun to protect me.

We worked on the exhibit until closing time, said our goodbyes to Petra, and left. As soon as we arrived home,

I threw all of Aiden's new clothes into the washer for a double wash. Although I was bursting inside to talk to Billy about the note and the ticket, I had to wait until Aiden went to bed. Billy had brought over a roasted chicken, mashed potatoes, and broccoli he had gotten from the super market, and we feasted. After I put the clothes into the dryer, we watched another of Aiden's movies. This was a documentary on baby animals. As cute as they all were, they didn't get my mind off what was in my purse. The movie ended, and I showed Aiden all his new clothes.

"I love them, Mommy! Look, Sheriff Billy. See the horse? And the spaceship? And Einstein, I love him!"

"Very cool," said Billy.

"Oh, I should have bought him some bigger pajamas, too."

Aiden looked struck and glanced at Billy, who just smiled. "No need. Aiden can keep my shirt for the duration of his recovery."

The biggest smile ever appeared on Aiden's face, and he launched himself into Billy's arms. "Thank you, Sheriff Billy!"

It was Aiden's turn to read, so he read to us from *The Chronicles of Narnia*. Afterward, we tucked him in, kissed him goodnight, and retired to the living room, where I could finally express what was bursting to come out for hours. But I decided to be cool about it.

"Um, so, did Derek come up with any fingerprints on my car door?"

"No, he said they were all smeared."

I handed Billy the note that he had crumpled up last time he saw it. "Kasey told me today that she used to call him Jonesy."

He sat up at that and read the note again. "That makes this pertinent then, doesn't it? Oh, I assume that Kasey didn't write it, right?"

"No, she didn't. Does the writing look familiar to you at all?"

Billy studied it. "No, not really. Should it?"

"Look again, Billy. Are you sure it doesn't look familiar?"

"No, I can't say it does."

"Then look at this." I handed him my ticket.

A grin spread across his face. "You got a ticket? In Coyote Moon?"

"No, Billy, right here in Rutledge."

He looked confused. "Derek gave you a ticket?"

"And thank goodness he did. Compare it to the note."

Billy held the note and the ticket in front of him. "I'll be!" he said. "They match perfectly, don't they?" He put them down and held one hand up to his mouth as he gazed off into the distance. "This explains a lot of things, doesn't it? Like why the fingerprints on the gun— except for Kasey's—were wiped off, and how he conveniently found the gloves in the top of the garbage. It also explains why his sister got to work early that day —he wanted to make sure she had an airtight alibi." He nodded. "It worked. Now what am I going to do? This barely even makes it circumstantial. There is not one shred of evidence that points to him."

"What about what he did to me today?"

"Today? Oh! You're right." He balled up his fists and looked protective, but then it passed. "That ties right in with it, doesn't it?" He thought for a minute more. "But it actually is a good thing. He's worried that I'm getting close."

"Or *I'm* getting close."

"Ha, yeah, unfortunately. But that's a good thing. That can be used against him. I'm not sure how yet, but I'll work it out."

"So Nick *stealing* his sunglasses was just a ploy in case Nick started getting suspicious—since they work so close together. Will you be bringing Nick back in now?"

"Oh, I couldn't do that, because it would tip Derek off that I was on to him. No, I'll have to give this some thought." He turned, put his hand on my shoulder, and looked at me seriously. "Good job, Lorry. You thought that note had significance right from the beginning. You've got a good head on your shoulders."

"Is that all you love me for is my brains?"

"No, not all." He leaned over, kissed me on the cheek, and stood up. "I need to leave early tonight to mull this over. I'll see you tomorrow."

"You'll go to Aiden's assembly with me, though, won't you?"

He looked off into the distance again and furrowed his brows. "Aiden's assembly. Oh, I forgot about that. That will depend on what happens tomorrow."

"Aiden will feel very disappointed if you don't go." I didn't mention that I'd feel disappointed, too.

"I'll do the best I can, Lorry. And Aiden will have to understand. And by the way, if he gets an idea in his head that he wants to wear my shirt to his performance tomorrow, it's all right with me. That should make him feel better if I'm not able to show up. But this case needs all my attention at this point to make sure that no one else gets hurt." He looked at me then and pulled me up off the couch so he could wrap his arms around me. "Like you. Or Aiden."

CHAPTER FIFTY-TWO

THE NEXT MORNING sped by. Because of the new sweatshirt, it only took an extra minute to help Aiden get dressed. He had picked out the Einstein sweatshirt to wear, and it went easily over the cast. That meant I could eat a full breakfast—two soft boiled eggs and toast—and have some coffee. So I was set—scared, but set. Knowing Derek was the murderer and was still out there somewhere running around scared me.

I buckled Aiden's seat belt, made sure Bingo's tail wouldn't get caught in the door, and then closed it and jumped into the front seat. After I dropped Aiden off at school, I drove back to the historical society, took my purse and Bingo out of the car, and locked it. Then, chicken that I am, I walked around the building and came in the front door.

"I'll be right there," called Petra.

"No need. It's only me," I said as I closed the jingling door behind me.

"Why'd you come in the front?" asked Petra. "You're not double parked again, I hope."

"No, I was, um, a little nervous about going in

241

through the back."

Petra chuckled. "I thought you might be, so I checked back there when I came in. The coast is clear!"

I walked to her office and put my arms out to hug her. "Oh, Petra. You did that for me?"

She put out her left arm in a stop gesture. "No unnecessary sentimentality, Lorry. I just did it."

"All right. Well, thank you then, my friend." I bent over in a deep bow. Bingo jumped up on her, got his required petting, and then ran upstairs to snuggle with Rocky.

"So what's on the agenda for today? Anything exciting?"

"Oh! I forgot to tell you that Aiden is giving a poetry reading tonight at his school. There is a big assembly planned. Any chance you and Mason can make it?"

"Ahh. Mason got tickets for a show in Coyote Moon. He'll be disappointed. Me, too. Well, next time, I guess. I'll have to tell Aiden to let me know in advance next time. I'm not going to tell you that, because you'll probably forget!"

"What? You think I'm senile or something? I just have a bad memory—especially with so much going on."

"Yeah, yeah. Anyway, I have to get back to work now." She turned and started typing something on her keyboard.

I walked back into my office and sat down in front of the computer, which I turned on. A couple of minutes later, I checked my email and found one from Martha. It said the new computer, the new computer desk, and the table for the scanner would arrive today. Oh! I had forgotten all about the box in the back of my car.

"Petra?"

"Yes, Lorry?"

"Any chance you can help me with something right now? It will only take a minute."

"Yeah, sure. What do you need?"

"I have a box in the back of my car. Will you hold the door open for me?"

"Yeah, go ahead. I'll be right there."

Tentatively, I walked to the back, and when I got to the curtained closet, I held my breath and pulled back the curtain. The ladder was there, Rocky's cat box that needed cleaning, and some other random stuff, but no assailant. Sighing deeply, I opened the back door, walked out to the car, opened the back, and took out the box. By that time, Petra was at the back door holding it open for me.

"What's that?" she asked as I walked by her.

"A scanner."

"What's it for?"

"Didn't Martha tell you about my new project?"

"New project? Oh! Finally! She's been talking about scanning all the documents forever."

"Yeah, now that she's learned to type, she won't need me to do that anymore." I put the box down and returned to my desk.

At ten o'clock, they delivered the computer and new furniture. The two men were very accommodating and put it exactly where I wanted it upstairs. They even brought up the scanner box for me. Although it wasn't heavy, I didn't want to carry it up the stairs. Those stairs had a reputation, and I didn't want to end up another statistic.

I spent the rest of the morning and part of the afternoon setting up what I knew of the computer and rearranging the furniture. Although I had the men put it where I thought I wanted it, I had to change it a dozen times just to be *absolutely* sure. In the end, the desk where I would sit was next to the stairway with the scanner to the right of the desk. That way, I could hear when the bell on the front door jingled and could run down before Petra had to get up. The computer was set up on the right-hand portion of the desk so I could lean over and look down the stairs toward the exhibit area. I wasn't sure what good that would do me, but it seemed like a good idea at the time.

As I sat at the desk admiring all my hard work changing the order of things a dozen times, Rocky jumped into my lap and started purring. And *that* would be an added bonus to working up here! Bingo was at my feet, Rocky was in my lap, and I was feeling happy. So I sneezed to seal the deal.

CHAPTER FIFTY-THREE

AIDEN CAME IN after school and as we worked on the exhibit together, he chattered on happily about a new friend he had at school. He said his friend was named Sage, and his family had just moved to town from the east coast. The name sounded familiar to me, but I couldn't place it.

At five o'clock, I still hadn't heard from Billy. I called the office, and they said he was out and had been all day. Then I called his cell, but it went to voice mail. So he had either turned it off, or he was on the phone. My guess was that he had turned it off. I didn't know if it was Derek's day off or not, but maybe Billy was following him to make sure he didn't do anything else bad. After leaving a message, I suggested to Aiden that we go out to dinner before his big performance.

As we drove to Grizelda's Bar and Grill, Aiden asked, "Is Sheriff Billy meeting us for dinner before my performance?"

"I don't think so, kiddo. He's been tied up all day with something urgent."

"He's going to my performance, though, isn't he?"

"Honestly, Aiden, I don't know. Last I heard, he said he would go if he could, but he wasn't certain."

"Oh," said Aiden, clearly disappointed.

We pulled into the parking lot and walked to the front door. Except for a scrungy bar at the other side of town called Petey's, Grizelda's was the only place to get a decent meal in Rutledge. *Decent* being debatable. But we didn't have time to go anywhere else. The outside of the building was painted pink—what possessed them to do that was beyond me—and they had two big windows in the front.

Inside, it smelled like hamburgers and onions. Straight ahead was the bar, with two- and four-person tables scattered around the room. Still hoping for Billy to call, we sat at a four-person table. When I was in high school and the owners called this place Grizelda's Pizza Parlor, I got kicked out for laughing too loud. Weren't those the days!

I kept checking my cell phone, but to no avail. Aiden ordered a fish sandwich, and I ordered a Reuben. Luckily, they served us quickly, because we still had to make a stop at home before we drove to the school. Aiden wanted to taste my Reuben, but he spit out the sauerkraut.

"But you like kraut dogs."

"It's different," he said and went back to eating his fish sandwich.

When we finished, we drove home so Aiden could get changed for the assembly. "Do you know what you want to wear, Aiden?"

"You know, Mommy," he said matter-of-factly, "those new sweatshirts you got me are all very nice, but they're so big."

I knew where he was going with this, but I let it continue as if I didn't. He didn't know that Billy had already said it was all right for him to wear the sheriff's shirt. "Yes, you're right. But that's so they can accommodate your cast."

"I just don't think they're appropriate for my performance tonight. They look messy."

"Would you like to cut off the sleeve on one of your more fitted ones, then?"

"No, what I would like to do is wear the sheriff's shirt that Sheriff Billy loaned me. Do you think he would mind?" He raised his eyebrows and looked at me expectantly.

Gathering him up in my arms, cast and all, I said, "Billy said it was all right if you wore it! So go for it, little man!"

He wiggled out of my arms, and as he ran for his bedroom, he said over his shoulder, "I do believe you were having one over on me, Mom!"

I helped him put the shirt on, and he put on the matching pants he had worn for Halloween. After tucking the shirt inside the pants—although it hung on him because Billy was so big and he was so small—I had to say that he looked stunning. "What a handsome boy I have!"

When we walked out the door, I told Bingo to guard the house, and we jumped into the car. We were running slightly behind. It was difficult finding a parking spot at the school because so many other cars were there, but I found one not that far from the school entrance.

"Mommy, hurry, we're late!"

"No, Aiden, it's five to six, we have five minutes to get you to your classroom."

Aiden had to be there at 6:00, and the program didn't start until 6:30. The school wasn't that big, and his classroom not that far. I locked the car, and then we walked into the school much faster than I would have liked because Aiden was so excited to get there.

After dropping him off in his classroom, I walked down the long hallway toward the auditorium. It had an inside and an outside entrance. The inside entrance had two eighth-grade students telling everyone that the inside door was reserved for the students who were performing and that the general public had to use the outside entrance. That didn't make sense to me as they also had a separate door to the stage right there. In addition, I had never thought of myself as "general," but I walked outside anyway.

As I exited the building so I could walk around to the other entrance, I checked my cell phone again. No call from Billy. Where was he? Then I turned it to vibrate and stuck it back into my purse. Many people milled around outside, and I made my way through the crowd heading toward the entrance. Then I heard someone call my name.

"Lorry! Lorry!"

The voice sounded familiar but out of place, and I didn't know who it was. Then someone placed a hand on my shoulder, and I turned around. It was Sam Kohn, my best friend from high school, and she had a little girl, about four years old, by one hand and a boy, Aiden's age, by the other.

"Sam!" I wrapped my arms around her in a tight hug. "Are you visiting?"

She lifted her eyebrows and smiled at me. "No. We're living here now."

"But, but I thought you had *a sign from the universe* that you shouldn't move here?" I didn't exactly know what a sign from the universe was, but last time I had seen her she had mentioned it.

"Yes, but things change, don't they?" She had a twinkle in her eye, and I knew just what she meant. "Anyway, let me introduce you to my children. This is my daughter, Willow, and my son, Sage."

"Nice meeting both of you. Wait. Sage? You're Aiden's new friend, right?"

The boy nodded his head enthusiastically. "Yeah, I really like Aiden."

"He likes you, too." Sam's daughter's name of Willow sounded perfect. I always thought of Sam as tall and willowy. And the daughter looked just like her with black hair and blue eyes. Sage had dark brown hair and dark eyes. I had never met Sam's husband, but maybe he looked like him.

"Where's Aiden now?" asked the boy, looking around.

"He's going to be performing! He was so excited about it."

Hesitantly, Sam asked, "Are you here *with* anybody?"

"No, darn it. My boyfriend had to work tonight. A big case. He's the county sheriff. I was hoping he'd get here in time"—I looked at my watch—"but it doesn't look like it."

"Would you like to sit with us?"

"Sure! But I'd like to sit close to the front so I can see Aiden clearly."

Little Willow pulled on her mother's hand. "Mommy, I want to sit close to the front."

"Then it's settled! Let's go in."

We survived the crowded doorway and found seats in

the second row, just off center. It couldn't be any better. There was a short kid in front of me, so I could see the stage perfectly. I couldn't wait to see Aiden on stage.

The school auditorium was a large room with a stage in the front and basketball nets on each side that were currently pushed against the walls. There was an electronic scoring panel behind bars—to protect it from stray basketballs—on each side ten feet away from the baskets. The stage had two sets of beige curtains hanging from the top of what I could see of the stage to the floor. Although I could only see one set of the curtains now because they were closed, I knew about the second set because I had been in this auditorium before. Many times.

Sam and I chitchatted as we waited for the program to begin, and when the lights flashed, although I didn't know it at the time, I was about to see the performance of a lifetime.

CHAPTER FIFTY-FOUR

WITH THE LIGHTS turned down low, a spotlight appeared, and the principal of the school, Pamela Reilly, walked onto the center of the stage to start the show. She gave a short speech about Thanksgiving and that we should all be grateful for all of our many blessings. Then she introduced the kindergarten class who in unison sang a song about turkeys. It was very sweet. After Pamela introduced the first grade, they came out and did a very brief skit on the first Thanksgiving. All the kids were dressed up as Pilgrims or Native Americans. It wasn't very *politically correct*, but the kids were cute.

I thought I felt my cell phone vibrate in my purse, but if Billy was calling this late, it was too late. And I didn't want to miss a minute of the precious performances. I could call Billy back when the show was over.

Pamela came back onto the stage and said for the second through eighth grades, each class had selected two children to give a performance. That made me so proud! Aiden hadn't told me he was only one of two in the second grade who would perform. The first child who came out, though, wasn't Aiden, but a classmate of his. She was a little girl wearing a pink froufrou dress that a ballerina might wear. With pink tights and pink ribbons in her hair, she was darling. The interpretive dance she performed, with Thanksgiving lyrics to go with it, was awesome. She impressed me so much that I wanted to give her a standing ovation, but nobody else stood up, so neither did I.

Then Aiden appeared on stage looking confident and absolutely dapper in his sheriff's outfit. My heart almost burst with pride and joy. My son. He hadn't let me hear him practicing, so I had no idea what he was going to do.

"Ladies and gentlemen," he started, holding the black microphone to his mouth. "Tonight I will recite to you two short Thanksgiving poems." Then he gave the title and author of the first poem and began reciting. His performance was perfect, of course. It was a cute little poem about cooking the Thanksgiving turkey. When he finished, he gave the title and author of the second poem. He had just finished the first verse of the poem, another cute poem in the spirit and rhythm of *'Twas the Night before Christmas*, when total chaos erupted in the auditorium.

For me, it happened in slow motion. Aiden had a smile on his face that immediately evaporated when Derek, still dressed as a deputy, charged onto the stage with his gun drawn and pointed at Aiden. It looked like he was startled by Aiden looking like a miniature sheriff. I stood up with my hands on my face and screamed, "Aiden!"

Aiden didn't look at me, but Derek did, and his gun followed, aimed right at me. Aiden dropped the microphone, took two steps forward and gave Derek a kick in the side of the knee that might have been a football clipping foul if he had come from the back. At the same moment, several men, whom I hadn't noticed leaning against the walls, ran forward and held guns pointed right at Derek. Nick, the formerly suspended deputy, rushed from the other side of the stage with his gun drawn, and Billy bolted past Aiden—who was escaping on one hand and his knees behind the second curtain—and with one swift movement, knocked the gun out of Derek's hand and first put one handcuff on, and then turned him around and put the other one on. After that, Nick and Billy escorted him out through the side entrance of the stage.

The other men were still standing until Aiden appeared back on stage, the picture of serenity, and completely unruffled by what had just happened, announced the name and author of his second poem again, and started reciting. I was still standing, but Sam pulled me down beside her and started rubbing my arm to calm me. The men with the guns holstered their weapons—wherever their holsters were—and blended back into the walls. The crowd in the auditorium had been agitated and mumbling, and who could blame them, but Aiden wasn't into the second poem more than a few lines, before everyone in the audience was still.

When he finished, the crowd stood and applauded and went mad. Pamela came onto the stage, hugged Aiden to her, took the microphone from him, and said, "Considering what happened here tonight, and how lucky we are to have a sheriff who handled a dangerous situation so deftly, and not to mention a boy who risked his own life to save his mother, I think I will say that this officially concludes our assembly. Please go home now and be safe." Then she collapsed onto the stage, and

Aiden held her as tears streamed from her face.

Sam stood so I could scoot past her, and I ran up onto the stage to hug Aiden. That was for me. Then Aiden and I both wrapped our arms around Pamela to calm her. That was for her. See? I'm not completely self-centered. And now that I knew my boy was safe, I felt, well, almost invincible.

CHAPTER FIFTY-FIVE

PAMELA WAS TOUGH and recovered quickly. It was overwhelming for her to think about what *might* have happened. She thanked Aiden and me and exited stage right. Sam and her two children were waiting for us when we got off the stage. Sam hugged me and Sage hugged Aiden. Willow just hung onto her mother.

"What a mechayeh that everything turned out all right! Was that your boyfriend who handcuffed the guy with the gun?" Sam asked.

"Yes, that's him." I shook my head. "I don't know what might have happened if he hadn't been here." Looking at Aiden, I breathed deeply to keep from breaking out in tears. Suddenly, I needed to get home where I felt safe. Although I didn't know how soon I'd see Billy, I knew that when I did, it would be at home. "Sam, I've got to get out of here. Great to see you. Let's get together as soon as we can." I took Aiden's hand, started to walk away, then had a thought and turned back. "Sam, do you and Mark and the kids want to come to Thanksgiving tomorrow?"

"Thank you, Lorry, but we're driving to the valley to

Mark's folks' house."

I hugged her with one arm. "Hope to see you soon, Sam."

"Bye, Lorry! I'm glad you and Aiden are safe."

"Me, too," I said as I escorted him out of the auditorium.

We got to the car, I buckled Aiden into the back seat, and I drove home without thinking. When we got into the house and Bingo greeted us at the door, I sank down on the couch pulling Aiden with me. I enfolded him in my arms and, overcome with emotion, tears gushed out of me.

"Mommy, what's wrong? Why are you crying? We're safe now. Bingo wouldn't let anything bad happen to us now."

After kissing his cheek, I said, "Aiden, it's what *almost* happened. What *could* have happened. That's why I'm crying. I'm so grateful that you're okay and that everything turned out all right. It could have been horrendous." Shaking my head, I added, "I can't even think about it." Then I kissed him on the cheek again. "And you, up there on stage, protecting me." Giving him a quick hug, I held him at arm's length and made my voice sound stern. "Don't you ever do that again! You risked your life for me. I appreciate that, but I don't want you risking your own life to save mine. That's just not right."

"But, Mommy," he said, his blue eyes blinking innocently at me, "the gun was pointed at you, so I wasn't risking my life. If he had pointed it at me, I wouldn't have done that."

"Oh, Aiden!" I pulled him to me again and resumed crying. Leave it to Aiden to sort out the details like that.

When I recovered my senses and Aiden was squirming around wanting to get free, I stood up, picked up my purse from the floor where I had dropped it, and retrieved my cell phone. It had two text messages, both from Billy. The first one said *Take A and get out of there now!* The second one said *On way to Coyote Moon. Don't know when home.* Billy didn't usually abbreviate, but him being in a rush was understandable for both of these texts.

Bedtime came early for Aiden because *I* felt so tired. Thankfully, although it was my turn to read, Aiden volunteered to do the reading. But instead of sitting in a chair beside his bed, I lay down beside him with Bingo snuggled up beside me. And soon, I was asleep.

However, I didn't know that had happened until hours later, when I heard Billy's voice in my ear. "Come on, Lorry, come into the other room with me."

As I stood up in a sleepy haze, Billy helped me to the living room, where we both sat on the couch with Billy's arm tight around me. Whispering in my ear, he said, "I love you, Lorry."

I put my head on his shoulder and replied, "I love you, Sheriff Billy." Sometimes when I'm tired I mix things up. I only occasionally called him that, but Aiden always did. Still, I said it, and I'm not going to be ashamed of it or even regret it. My excuse, and it's a good one, is that I felt so tired—both emotionally and physically.

Billy chuckled and kissed my forehead. "Did you not get my message or just choose to ignore it?"

"Neither. I heard it come through, but I didn't read it until I got home. Then it was too late." Not wanting to cry again, I took a deep breath and tried to calm myself. "So what happened in Coyote Moon?"

"He confessed everything: the murder, wiping the

prints off the murder weapon, planting the gloves and then finding them, the anonymous phone call accusing John, assaulting you, and he didn't need to confess what happened tonight. There were more than a hundred witnesses. Are you okay? Is Aiden okay?"

"We're both okay, but Aiden is doing better than I am. I still can't believe he risked his life for me like that."

"But he didn't. He waited until the gun was pointed *at you.*"

"That's what *he* said. But it didn't feel like that." Taking another deep breath, I asked, "How did Derek end up at the school, anyway?"

"Oh, that was an unfortunate circumstance. Nick had been following him, and at some point Derek must have figured it out. He went into the Urgent Care Clinic, and Nick waited for him out front. But Derek went out the back door. When Nick realized what happened and called me, I had a suspicion he might come here. There were two choices: he had somehow left his car in the back, but he would have had to drive past Nick to leave, so I didn't think that was it. Or, he could have walked to where he was going to freak out. Since it seemed like everything was escalating, I chose the second. And the school being so close to the clinic, it seemed like the obvious choice. Plus, you know, he had threatened you and your family." Billy sighed, relieved that it worked out all right.

"Expecting the worst from Derek, I had already assembled a team who were ready. Then I called Pamela Reilly to warn her to cancel the performance, but she wasn't in her office. By the time we all got there, it had begun."

"Wow," was all I could say.

"Derek did something that I never expected, though, and that was my fault. He came still dressed in his uniform. And with that uniform, he was able to talk himself in past the kid at the stage door. Derek got to the stage less than a minute before we did." Billy sighed again and tightened his arm around me. "And you know the rest."

"Yes. Better than I would have liked, I'll tell you. I know it better than I would have liked."

CHAPTER FIFTY-SIX

THE FOLLOWING DAY, Billy arrived early looking happy. He had left so late the night before, after telling me the whole story, that I didn't know how he could not feel tired. I was tired, though, so I was very grateful that he had come over so early to help me set everything up for the big dinner.

Billy had brought a couple of big tables that we set up in the living room after moving the regular furniture to the sides of the room. He even brought a big tablecloth to put over them so they looked nicer. It was a holiday, after all. Billy also thought to bring chairs so everyone had a place to sit. And *everyone* was a lot.

We were expecting Petra, Mason, Petra's mother whom Billy had talked into coming, Bryan and Ryan, Zack, Nick and his girlfriend, and two last-minute additions were Martha and Hugo. All the people they had expected over Thanksgiving were one big group, and they had missed their first flight and wouldn't arrive until Friday. That made me so happy—not that the group missed their flight—but that Martha and Hugo would be at our Thanksgiving. I loved them both and was grateful to have them in my life. And that's what Thanksgiving was for.

By the time people started coming in at two o'clock, I was about ready to drop. So Billy donned my apron and continued getting everything prepared. He would make someone a good wife. I hoped that someone would be me. What a great guy he was.

When Mason, Petra, and her mother walked in, I noticed that Petra's mother was sporting a shiner. Her whole eye was black and partway closed. Petra's father had never hit her before according to Petra, but maybe things had changed. Since Billy is the one who talked her into coming, I knew he would feel bad about it. But there was nothing he could do, and maybe something good would come of it.

Everyone was there at three o'clock, and Billy and I and Petra—thank her weird little soul—put everything out on the table. We ate and ate and ate and stuffed our faces, just like you're supposed to do at Thanksgiving. When we all finished eating, Petra and Mason volunteered to clear the table. Then Billy got up and brought the pumpkin and apple pies in and set them on the table. Petra and Mason had brought the pie plates and the ice cream.

Then Billy surprised me by standing up. "Before we eat our dessert, I want to say something. I'm sure all of you have heard what happened yesterday, and how close I was to losing two of the most important people in my life, Lorry and Aiden." He stopped, blinked his eyes a couple of times, and looked first at me and then at Aiden. "It made me realize how much they mean to me and how important they are to me"—he hesitated a beat —"and that is more than words can say. And I know this will embarrass her, but I am going to do it anyway, because all of you are such important people in both of our lives, and I wanted you to be present when I did this." At that, Billy dropped to one knee beside my seat, and said, "Lorry, I'm madly in love with you and would like to spend the rest of my life with you and Aiden. Will you marry me?"

I didn't know what to say. Well, of course I knew what to say, but words had escaped me once again. All I could do was choke and nod, and then cough out a "yes." Everyone laughed and clapped, and Billy placed the ring on my finger and then kissed me on the lips.

Looking down at the ring, I laughed. Billy smiled, shrugged, and said, "It's all I could come up with so quickly." He had put a cigar band on my finger.

When he sat back down on his seat and started divvying up the pie, Aiden looked at Billy. "Sheriff Billy? Does that mean I can call you Daddy from now on?"

Billy looked at Aiden, thought for a second, nodded his head and said, "That's *Sheriff* Daddy to you!"

If you liked this book and feel so inclined, please leave a review on Amazon. Thank you! I appreciate it!

And if you'd like to know when the next Rutledge Historical Society mystery comes out, sign up for the mailing list: http://www.ralstonstorepublishing.com/mysteryL.html

Read the next book in the series: Rogues to Riches.

When a woman is murdered in front of the new 1950s murder exhibit, Lorry is convinced that the two murders are connected. But with a wedding to plan, who has time to find a murderer? Sassy, irreverent Lorry Lockharte, that's who.

Other books published by Ralston Store Publishing:

Time Travel Sweet Romance
Cowgirls in Time Series by Erica Einhorn
A Chill Wind
Wind Beneath My Wings
Against the Wind
The Healing Wind
Ride Like the Wind
Wind of Change
The Way the Wind Blows

Caregiving
The Journey that Matters by Jodie Lightener

Suspense
Darkness in the Light by J.K. Lincoln

India
Not My Guru by Parvati Hill

Women's Fiction/Reincarnation
Two Lifetimes, One Love by Thea Thaxton

Yoga Books
Bathroom Yoga
Airplane Yoga
Wheelchair Yoga
Essential Yoga on Horseback
Exercises for Therapeutic Riding

Kousins Kan't Kill